P9-CEB-218

19

Miahualin Garcia

The Vampire's
Beautiful Daughter

Books from Byron Preiss Visual Publications and
Atheneum Books for Young Readers:

LETTERS FROM ATLANTIS
by Robert Silverberg

THE DREAMING PLACE
by Charles de Lint

THE SLEEP OF STONE
by Louise Cooper

BLACK UNICORN
by Tanith Lee

CHILD OF AN ANCIENT CITY
*by Tad Williams and
Nina Kiriki Hoffman*

DRAGON'S PLUNDER
by Brad Strickland

WISHING SEASON
by Esther M. Friesner

THE WIZARD'S APPRENTICE
by S. P. Somtow

GOLD UNICORN
by Tanith Lee

BORN OF ELVEN BLOOD
*by Kevin J. Anderson and
John Gregory Betancourt*

THE MONSTER'S LEGACY
by Andre Norton

THE ORPHAN'S TENT
by Tom De Haven

MONET'S GHOST
by Chelsea Quinn Yarbro

THE VAMPIRE'S BEAUTIFUL DAUGHTER
by S. P. Somtow

THE VAMPIRE'S
BEAUTIFUL DAUGHTER

S. P. SOMTOW

Illustrated by Gary A. Lippincott

A Byron Preiss Book

Atheneum Books for Young Readers

THE VAMPIRE'S BEAUTIFUL DAUGHTER

Atheneum Books for Young Readers
An imprint of Simon & Schuster Children's Publishing Division
1230 Avenue of the Americas
New York, NY 10020

Cover painting by Gary A. Lippincott. Cover design by Brad Foltz
Edited by Keith R. A. DeCandido

Special thanks to Jonathan Lanman, Howard Kaplan, and John Betancourt.

First Edition
Printed in the United States of America
10 9 8 7 6 5 4 3 2 1

ISBN 0-689-31968-1

Library of Congress Card Catalog Number: 97-70080

For Somtow's Little Helpers:
Johnny, Victor, George, and Vanina

THE VAMPIRE'S
BEAUTIFUL DAUGHTER

CHAPTER ONE

My Own
Private Identity Crisis

They said to me: "Don't worry, Johnny, you'll never feel out of place where you're going, where cultural diversity is king." They said to me: "They have eighty-three languages in their school district. They have teriyaki burritos and Peking duck pizzas. They won't force you to be one thing or the other. You can be everything you want to be, and ought to be."

I said to them: "You must be joking. I watch TV too, you know. White cops beat up black motorists there. Vigilantes shoot kids for tagging on walls. They'll eat me alive."

They said to me: "It's a great opportunity. It's a dream come true."

I said to them: "It's a nightmare."

They said to me: "Movie stars! Talk shows! Lights, camera, action!"

I said to them: "Earthquakes. Floods. Riots."

There were a lot more of them than me, and when you're fifteen, you don't have much say in it anyway. So we got in the beat-up Caprice and set sail for Hollywood. By the time we got there, the Caprice had become a BMW, and our jeans and T-shirts were in the trunk, and we were duded out in polyester—the guys at least, me and my grandfather—my mother and my sister stuck with the hippie look.

We moved out of Wall, South Dakota, you see, because we suddenly got rich.

Five years ago, my grandpa started talking. He talked before, of course, but only like, "Pass the salt," or "This is a damn fine piece of steak." All my life, he would only say one or two sentences a day, and then, just like that, he turns into Mr. Motormouth. My mom, always the hardworking anthropologist, wrote it all down, and you've seen the book in the front of every chain bookstore in every shopping mall, the one with the Sitting Bull clone on the cover.

That's my grandfather. My father vanished in a puff of smoke when I was three. My little sister Astrid's father is Norwegian. He left too.

I've heard many theories about my dad. For example, that he pledged a sundance one summer, gouged himself too deeply and died of gangrene. That's a stupid theory. Why wouldn't someone have taken him to the hospital? Or that he had a multiple personality, and one day one of his other selves took over permanently, and he's now selling insurance in Florida. Yeah, right. I think he just left because he had enough of being not quite one thing and not quite the other.

Actually, I *really* think he left because of me.

That's why I don't use his last name. I'm still too mad at him.

I don't use my mother's either, because if I say I'm Johnny Shapiro, people just say, "You don't *look* Jewish."

I picked the name Raitt out of the phone book when we arrived in Los Angeles. I like the sound of Johnny Raitt. It rhymes with Bonnie Raitt. Around here, though, I've had to start listening to other kinds of music. Like the Senseless

2

Vultures, who are very big in my school, the Claudette Colbert High School, which sits on top of the Santa Monica Mountains, straddling the 818 and 310 area codes—the old money of Beverly Hills to the south, the new money of Encino to the north.

Our money was *real* new. Our house was in Encino.

It wasn't a big house, but it was south of the Boulevard so it cost about twenty times what our house in South Dakota cost. It was halfway up the hill, so I could walk to school, which was embarrassing because everyone else drove.

I wanted to have all the things all the other kids had, but my mom said we had to wait for the "on pub" money.

I said, "But it's a bestseller! They owe you a million bucks or something!"

She said, "Don't ask me, honey; I'm new at this."

Then she went off to a *shabbes* at her aunt's house. I hated all Mom's relatives—I'd never had to deal with them before—and they treated me like a freak. So Friday nights I spent with my grandpa.

Wasn't that much fun, because he had stopped talking again. I don't think he liked Encino very much.

I guess I didn't mind it. I belonged with the Peking duck pizza and the teriyaki burrito; and in my school, people really didn't mind that at all. There were all kinds of mutts at Claudette Colbert, and if I started to tell anyone about my complex origins, they always said, "That's nothing! You should hear about *my* identity crisis." Having an identity crisis was considered cool. It was good to blend in at first, but after a week it was a pain to be just another identity crisis dude. All day long you hear these warm fuzzy messages telling you to be content with who you are, but they never really reach the anger inside of you. So I gritted my teeth, started saying "like" at least once in every sentence, and buckled down to being just another angst-ridden teen-ager in the privileged 'burbs.

Okay, it wasn't that bad. As long as I didn't admit to listening to country music now and then, I was pretty safe. The pierced-nipple crowd sat in the back row, and preps peppered the front; people like me were comfortably in the middle, and didn't have to participate too much in class. Some of the classes were downright interesting, like the "History of Womankind" unit that included stuff about Neo-lithic matriarchies and Wiccan, and where we studied how women made all the political decisions among the Mo-hawk—even I hadn't known that. It was rumored that Mrs. Chapman, the hyper–politically-correct social studies teacher, was a witch herself. She sure bewitched all the guys in her class.

Then there was Dr. Kyril, the computer teacher—or, as he called himself, our cyberspace expedition leader. His wife was a major scream queen, the star of *The Beast That Threw Up Schenectady*. Maybe you've seen that one. I've seen it four times. She takes a lot of showers in that movie. She has to, to get rid of all the gore.

The kids themselves, too, were cool. Every one of them had an identity crisis worse than mine, it seemed. Joel Her-skovitz, who sat next to me, had just announced on *Jerry Springer* that he was saving up for a sex change when he turned eighteen. Tanya Tan was suing a big movie director to acknowledge her as his kid, and was being countersued for libel. About half the kids had problems of that nature. The other half were actors, or acted like they were actors. You wouldn't believe how many people have been in a cereal commercial for three seconds.

My second week at Claudette Colbert High School, I met someone whose identity crisis blew mine right out of the water. She was as pale as a wheatfield in winter, and she wore black. Her hair was jet black, too, though I guess it could've been dyed. Her eyes were wide and hypnotic. She seemed more like a special effect than a human being—I mean, like your life is a color movie and there's this halo of black-and-whiteness that surrounds her. You've seen that effect on MTV, but she *lived* it. Her name was Rebecca Teppish, and she was more mixed up than I could ever be.

At least my father was a human being.

Rebecca's father was a vampire.

CHAPTER TWO

REBECCA TEPPISH

Maybe you didn't catch that. Or maybe you think I'm joking.

No way.

I'll tell you how I know.

Rebecca showed up at one of the more embarrassing moments in my life. It was in Mrs. Chapman's class, and it was the day we were supposed to hand in our Cultural Diversity papers. We were supposed to do these little essays about our roots. I didn't hand one in.

"I'm sorry," I said, "but, well, like, my computer's down."

That was the one excuse all teachers around here seemed to commiserate with. Everyone in my class would hand in these desktop published papers with fancy covers and artwork pasted in from an encyclopedia CD-ROM. I was the only one I knew who didn't have a computer at all. That was another thing on the list of stuff to get when the "on pub" payment came through. Next door, a sixth-grade dweeb named Mikey had a Power PC 8100 with 36 megs of RAM, but he only used it for role-playing games. Sometimes I was able to bum the use of it from him, but I always had to bribe him with baseball cards, milk caps, or candy bars.

"Down?" said Mrs. Chapman. "That's what you said last time."

"Uh, it's the hard drive," I said.

"Oh dear," she said. It almost hurt me to lie to her. "I know what. I'll lend you this piece of software." She rummaged in her purse and found an old disk, covered with cookie crumbs, wiped it on her caftan, and handed it to me. "I swear by this. It's magic. Your hard disk'll be good as new. Bring in the paper tomorrow."

It was going to be tough to get out of this one. "But I have an Amiga," I said in desperation. "They're not compatible."

"Well, Johnny," said Mrs. Chapman, "then you're just going to have to do it orally."

Half the class moaned, the rest started to laugh.

"You can't," I said. "I don't do oral."

"We're talking, aren't we?"

"Yes, but like, I'm totally nonverbal. I'm right-brained. Too much verbalization lowers my self-esteem."

"Give me a break, Johnny," she said. Everyone laughed at me.

Then Mrs. Chapman did something so embarrassing, I thought I would have to stay home sick for the rest of the school year.

"Actually," she said, "we all have quite a head start on Johnny's roots." She rummaged in that purse again—a *huge* purse, more like a shopping bag—and pulled out a copy of *Renewing the Hoop: The Philosophy of Joseph Hides-from-Bears, As Told to His Daughter-in-Law Irena Shapiro.* "Johnny has one of the most interesting family histories I know about, and a lot of it is in this book." She put on her reading glasses and began flipping through it, and I saw that there wasn't enough room to hide under my desk, so I kind of stared at the floor. "It must have been fascinating," she said, "spending the early years of your life at the Pine Ridge Reservation. Johnny's grandfather writes about driving out into the badlands and spending weeks out there, communing with the spirits and having visions, while you and your mother slept in the back of an old Chevy Caprice."

"I don't remember," I said.

Then the rest of the class actually got interested, and they started begging me to talk, which really got to me. Finally I said, "I'm only twenty-five percent Lakota, and I'm twenty-five percent Polish, and fifty percent Jewish, and leave me alone."

"But that's just fascinating," Mrs. Chapman said relentlessly.

"It's not fascinating. It's a pain in the ass."

The punkers in the back row began applauding.

I said, "You shouldn't make me talk about this if I don't want to."

"But just think," Mrs. Chapman said, "you're part of a chain of being that sweeps across the world, and back through time. . . . What wonderful stories you must have heard from your grandfather, and from your great-grandparents."

"Yeah. Well, one set of my great-grandparents was massacred at Wounded Knee. Two more sets were gassed at Auschwitz. The fourth set got trampled to death by Cossacks." I realized that I was about to lose it completely. Tears were forming in my eyes, but I buried my head under a pile of books on my desk.

Mrs. Chapman saw that she'd gone too far—she's a wonderful teacher, really, she just pushed the buttons too hard—but then she started to tell me about this wonderful Teen Identity Crisis Support Group that met after school every Thursday at the mall, and I totally wanted to die.

But you can't stare at a piece of wood veneer forever,

and after a while I kind of sneakily started to sit back up again. My eyes were still blurry but that was the first time I saw Rebecca Teppish, standing in the doorway with a bundle of books under her arm. She must have seen the whole thing.

I told you how pale she was, but pale doesn't begin to describe it. She wasn't beautiful exactly, but she had a way of looking at you. She had really big eyes. But you couldn't really tell what color they were. Sometimes they were purple, and sometimes they were deep blue. She was kind of fragile looking, too.

She sort of tiptoed into the room and looked over the whole scene. It was tense. Then she said to me, "Dude, you think you have it bad. *My* father's a vampire."

Everyone started laughing, and I didn't feel so stupid after all.

Especially when she took the empty seat next to me. The one that had been empty all week, because everyone else in Mrs. Chapman's class had been friends, or enemies, whatever, since middle school, and no one knew who I was.

"Kids," said Mrs. Chapman, "this is Rebecca Teppish."

"And since we're doing genealogy," Rebecca said softly, "I'm half Romanian, half Irish." I got a faint whiff of her CK1. She wore a silver ankh around her neck, and that, I knew from my mom, was the ancient Egyptian symbol of life.

"Actually," she said, "it's not silver. It's platinum. My father wouldn't approve of silver."

"You're a telepath?"

"Not really. But after a while it gets so you can read people."

"Cool," I said. "What's your sign?"

We both laughed. "Actually, I was born on Halloween."

"Me too," I said.

"We're soul mates," she said softly.

Then Mrs. Chapman made us turn to another chapter in her book—the one on shamanism in Native American cultures. I live with that stuff all day long, so I started to drift away. But now and then, I couldn't help being aware of Rebecca, sitting perfectly still, the faintest smile on her lips, staring straight ahead, like she wasn't even breathing.

My little breakdown was an embarrassing thing that wouldn't go away, though. At lunchtime, people avoided me. Or stared at me. It wasn't a hostile thing. They were just full of curiosity, wanting to ask me questions, maybe even feeling sorry for me. But the last thing I needed was a dose of warm, fuzzy Californian empathy.

Claudette Colbert is an open campus, so lunch is pretty sparsely attended. There's a pizza place and several hamburger places down the hill a ways. The school cafeteria is not that bad, though. But yeah, they do have teriyaki burritos there.

I had a whole long table to myself, and I got ready to mope. I stared into my militantly healthy sesame chicken Caesar salad. I don't know when she arrived. She had this uncanny knack of moving so quietly that you couldn't even hear her in the back of your mind.

I just knew that her hand was brushing against my hand. Very lightly. Almost like the wind. A cold wind. Like back in Wall. A breath of snow. "Hi, Johnny," she said. I'd never told her my name, so she must have taken the trouble to find out.

"Thanks for the wisecrack," I said. "You kind of helped defuse the situation."

"Oh, that," she said, smiling. "But that wasn't a wisecrack, you know." She had a hint of some foreign accent. I couldn't place it. "It's the plain truth. Sometimes the truth can be its own disguise."

I laughed. She made me nervous, I'll admit. Not just my

11

raging hormones either. Everything she said gave me the sense of skirting the edge of something really dangerous.

"You're not eating?" I said.

"I brought lunch," she said. She had a tote bag—black—and she took out a Timmy Valentine lunch box. Scrawled in silver marker on the box was the name T-E-P-E-S. "Yeah, the spelling," she said. "I had it anglicized when I registered for school. At my last school, everyone kept pronouncing it 'teeps'." Inside, there was a plastic bottle—the kind they have in blood banks—and it was full of a red liquid.

"That's very funny," I said. "Cranberry juice, I bet."

"Grape, actually. Want some?" I said no. Not that I thought for a moment it was blood. But you know. It was the nervous thing. She really had it down.

"If that's all you're going to have," I said, "you might want to see an anorexia specialist."

"Hey," she said, "you need a friend, I need a friend. We could go sign up for that support group. Or we could turn to each other for support. At least we have the same birthday."

"Come to my birthday party?"

"Only if you come to mine."

"So your dad's a vampire? At least you *have* a dad."

"I guess," she said. And stared off into space somewhere.

What was she thinking of? There are people in the world who think they're vampires. I know, I saw it on *Montel*. Plus there was a *Hard Copy* segment about it. I'd never heard of someone who thought they were half a vampire, but being half of something was a concept I could really relate to.

Finally, she said, "I guess you don't believe me."

"You have to admit," I said, "it's tough to swallow."

"So, you want to study together tonight? I haven't written my roots paper either . . . I'll write yours and you can write mine. We can say the wildest things, and if she complains, we'll do a political correctness guilt trip on her. . . ."

"Sure," I said. I couldn't believe my luck.

12

"Here's the address."

"I don't have a car yet. I will, of course, once Halloween rolls around." Then I looked at the address and realized she lived only a few blocks from me, at the very summit of the hill, where Mulholland Drive meets Tirgoviste Lane.

"Hey, don't worry about it! Why drive when you can fly?"

"What are you talking about?"

"I'll show you. After it gets dark. This town is a lot more interesting after midnight. You'll see, I promise."

CHAPTER THREE

My Wacky Family

I couldn't get to Rebecca's house until almost nightfall. I had to deal with my grandpa; Mom was away for the week, gathering data on pre-Columbian artifacts in Mexico. She'd probably end up falling for an Aztec warrior, or something.

Grandpa was getting ready for a big autograph party at the Beverly Center that weekend. His editor, Janice, was at her wits' end because he wouldn't talk. I had to take the call. Long distance, New York; it was long after office hours in New York, too, so I knew she was worried out of her mind. I could imagine it now, a long line of fans at the fanciest mall in Los Angeles, stretching all the way down the bookstore to the entrance to the Hard Rock Café, and the man won't dispense any pearls of wisdom—they'll probably think he's faking it—or that my mom made up the whole thing— you know, the New Age self-help version of Milli Vanilli.

"What does it take?" she said.

"I don't know," I said. "Maybe a big family crisis of some

kind." That was what sparked off the last big talkfest: when Astrid's dad walked out on us and went back to Norway.

"Look, Johnny," said Janice. I walked around the kitchen with the cordless, trying to find something to feed Astrid when she came home from her karate class. "Maybe this is a bit manipulative, but do you think you could engineer some kind of family crisis? Try to kill yourself, or something? Teen suicide's always a good issue."

I don't even think she was joking. "How much will you pay me?" I said. "On second thought, talk to my agent."

"You don't have an agent," she said.

Bingo! I pulled out the Thai chicken salad that we'd picked up from the deli on Ventura. "You know I can just borrow an agent from one of my friends in school," I said.

She laughed. "Touché," she said. "You're good at this. Your mother should fire the William Morris Agency and use you. But please—try to get your grandfather in a talking mood. I beg you. If you do, I'll take you out to Le Dome for dinner when I'm in town for the Oscars."

"Oscars?"

"Didn't you know? Tygh Simpson of the Senseless Vultures is optioning your grandpa's book. Wants to use it as a vehicle for a comeback. You know, what with the big success of *Dances with Wolves*."

"But Grandpa's book doesn't have a plot," I said, then slugged down my kiwi-guava cocktail and hunted around for some good old cholesterol.

"Oh, they don't care about that. They just like the title. Besides, they have a plot already—it's one of those white-man-rapes-prairie-but-learns-meaning-of-life plots, a very feel-good story, I hear—and they just want to use your grandpa's book title and graft some of his brilliant aphorisms into it . . . maybe even give him a cameo as the wise old man, especially since they can't very well resurrect Chief Dan George."

16

I finally found my beef: a big old hunk of pemmican from the supply we'd brought over from South Dakota. Bit into it hard. That gamey, fruity, eye-smarting flavor just blows you away.

"Cool," I said. "So how do I fit in?"

"We need a few good sound bites. Tygh's PR people want to get him on *Hollywood Tonight*. Can you coax him into it?"

"What about the on pub payment?" I said sneakily. "Mom's not good with money. She spends it as fast as she gets it."

"You sweet-talk your grandpa," she said, "and I'll cajole the publishers. That shiny car for your sixteenth is at stake, Johnny!"

"Oh," I said. "Okay."

Half an hour before Astrid gets home, I thought. Half an hour with Grandpa, half an hour to settle Astrid down, then off to Castle Dracula. . . .

Grandpa does not live in the house at all. He prefers the garage. He has covered the concrete floor with buffalo robes, and hung a deerskin tentflap on the doorway, just behind the washer-dryer.

I usually had to wait behind the flap until he kind of sensed my presence, but I didn't have much time so I just went in. *"Tunkashila,"* I said, which is what he likes to be called, but it just means Grandpa in Lakota. "The publishers want you to talk again."

I don't think my grandfather is really descended from Sitting Bull. If it's true, it's him along with about a thousand other people. But he sure looks like the old photographs of Sitting Bull, especially when one of those moods come over him. He sat in the middle of the garage, smoking a pipe, and I sort of crawled in and sat across from him. The room smelled of leather, tobacco, and pemmican.

"Na," he said, handing me the pipe.

17

I puffed, said *"Ku,"* and handed it back. "But you know Mom will get mad if she finds out you've been letting me smoke again." I started coughing. Actually, she probably wouldn't be too mad about it, seeing as it was only a drag or two for the sake of tradition. She might draw the line at peyote.

"I do talk," he said.

"I know, but I think they mean like, *talk.* As in talk shows, talk radio, press interviews, pressing the flesh . . . you know. Being a celebrity."

"Is there a family crisis?"

"I'm in love with a vampire's daughter."

Of course, I wasn't in love yet. I was attracted, sure. But I wanted to say something to get my grandfather's attention.

"This *winchinchala,*" he said, "is she real?"

"Of course not, *Tunkashila.* She's lost in a fantasy world, dresses all in black, probably files her teeth, though I've never seen her smile, so I don't know. But you know, I'm going over to the mansion tonight, so I'll give you a full report."

"Well, don't get any ideas," he said.

"What do you mean?"

"About becoming a vampire yourself."

"Grandpa, it's some kind of big joke."

"Look. You're gonna be sixteen soon. You never had a chance to go on a vision quest, never had a chance to learn your true name, who you're really gonna be. Didn't want a bar mitzvah, either, so you're missing out on every flavor of initiation. You have to tune the heartstrings before you can sing. I wish you'd have never given up fancy dancing. You were the star of the powwow. It's all important, you know. Yeah, yeah, you'll tell me this is the nineties, none of these formalities really matters now. But one way or another you're gonna have to stop being a child. I don't want you choosing to be a vampire. I mean, if you must, you must,

18

but it's not a good thing. Man was made to be a child, grow up, make love, make babies, grow old, go back to nurture Mother Earth, you know that. Those vampires, they think they've broken the hoop, so they can go on forever. But there's a price they have to pay, believe me. *Hechitu welo!*"

"That's great, Grandpa!" I hugged him. "That's just what Janice wants you to do this weekend."

I must have said the wrong thing, because he stopped talking. Handed me the pipe one more time, took it back, then started sort of humming to himself and rocking back and forth. Then he began to sing in a wheezy, wavery sort of voice. My Lakota sucks, so I only caught a couple of words, like *akichita*, which means "warrior."

The last thing I wanted to hear was a lecture on how I needed to find myself, anyway. I went back to the kitchen just in time to see my little sister's karate car pool pull up. She was wearing some kind of ninja outfit, and she was just undoing her shaggy blond hair when I went into the living room with her culturally diverse, low cholesterol post-karate snack.

"So," I said, "did you kill anyone today?"

"Where's Mom?" she said, turning on the television. It was MTV, and it was an old Senseless Vultures video—*real* old, maybe a couple of years. Watching it, I couldn't imagine them collaborating with Grandpa at all.

"She went to Mexico," I said.

"Oh, no!" said Astrid, and she started bawling her eyes out.

"Are you okay?" I said, and sat down next to her. The music video continued to play. It showed a boy and a girl kissing, floating down from the ceiling on a plastic cloud. Kind of corny. I tried putting my arms around Astrid, but she didn't want to be touched.

"I feel terrible. I'm having my period," she said.

"Oh," I said. *What timing*, I thought.

"I've never had one before! What am I going to do? How do you use those things?"

"Well, calm down. This is kind of outside my experience. And I know you don't want to talk to one of Mom's cousins—"

"No way."

"Hey, I'm going over to a friend's house tonight. We're just going to study, but . . . well, she'll be sixteen soon. Maybe she can—"

"Johnny's got a girlfriend." She giggled. "This I have to see."

"She's not my girlfriend yet," I said. "But hey—I bring over my little sister for some good old woman talk, she'll have to conclude that I am one hell of a sensitive male and like, in touch with my feminine side."

"Yeah." Astrid grinned. "Girls like that."

"Get ready, then. Don't worry about your period. This is the nineties. We'll cope."

"Thanks, bro," she said, and kissed me on the cheek. "You *are* sensitive."

It took Astrid an hour to get dressed, which was the real reason it was almost nightfall by the time we got to Castle Dracula. . . .

CHAPTER FOUR

INTERVIEWED BY A VAMPIRE

We had to stop to get a box of "those things." I kind of thought that Rebecca might have some, but Astrid insisted that it would be bad manners to show up—uninvited—*and* expect free tampons. We went down to the Alpha Beta at the bottom of the hill—we used our Rollerblades to save time—but when we got there it turned out that the karate kid was too chicken to buy them herself.

One guess as to who ended up not only taking them up to the counter, but shelling out, while Sis stood with her head buried inside a gothic-punk fan magazine.

Rollerblading uphill was a lot harder, but we managed it by taking the little sidewinding streets, which aren't as steep.

The place was big, but it was hardly Castle Dracula. It was one of those Spanish-style estates, with a bunch of fountains, statues, and oleander hedges along a driveway that led to a portico with fake Ionic columns. The gate had opened automatically for us—some kind of security system I guess—

and we wandered around the grounds for a while, not knowing which doorbell to ring.

There was an Olympic-size pool, and if you stood at the edge of the pool you could see all the way down to the Valley, and you could see all the other pools, too, all sizes and shapes, glistening down the hillside like pieces of amethyst in the setting sun. It was beautiful up here, no smog—you could see clear to Malibu maybe. Astrid was oohing and aahing at it all, and then, all of a sudden, Rebecca was there.

"You snuck up on us!" I said.

She laughed. "Indians do not have a monopoly on sneaking up," she said. I frowned, so maybe she got worried about whether I'd be offended at the word *Indian*. That happens all the time.

"I couldn't care less what words you use," I said automatically.

"Are you a telepath?" she said.

Wow. Big, heavy dose of déjà vu here. Suddenly I almost believed her story about her dad being a vampire. Sometimes, people think you read their minds, but it's just that they're so predictable.

"This is my sister, Astrid," I said. "She might need your help." I started to whisper in her ear. I don't know why, really. I mean, it wasn't as if I knew something Astrid didn't know.

In any case, Rebecca's face darkened. Not literally, but you could tell there was something peculiar going on inside her brain. "Sure, Astrid," she said, "I'll tell you what you need to know." She took Astrid by the hand and we started to go toward the house.

We went in through a french door by the pool. She told me to sit and wait. It was a kind of parlor. Looked much more like Castle Dracula here than you'd have guessed from the outside: frayed, stuffed furniture with gilded legs, dusty

24

portraits of pissed-off-looking ancestors, and a grand piano covered with cobwebs.

"Come on, Astrid." Then she thought of something; she went to the credenza beneath one particularly severe-looking painting, a woman in a mile-high wig and ruffles, and she opened a drawer and took out two amulets—ankhs, like the one she was wearing. She put one around Astrid's neck, and one around mine.

"These ones are silver," she said. "As long as you're in this house, whatever you do, don't take them off."

Then she, Astrid, and the box of "those things" disappeared down the corridor. I started to get nervous. Rebecca was really taking all this vampire stuff very seriously. I fingered the ankh around my neck. It was cool to the touch. I sat down in one of those huge armchairs, and looked around.

There were a few typical Hollywood things. On one wall there was a signed photograph of teen star Timmy Valentine—now there was something people would pay a lot for. Then there was a bronze statuette of Bela Lugosi on the coffee table, which was covered with a purple velvet drape. A crystal chandelier hung from the ceiling. And some of the furniture was draped in, like, black plastic sheets.

I whistled. How long could it take for a girl to tell another girl the facts of life? Especially when the other girl was as precocious as my sister Astrid, and didn't need to know the facts of life exactly, just needed a little fine-tuning?

After a while, I stopped feeling nervous. Soon, I'd be alone with the most intriguing girl in my school. That was worth feeling happy about. I put my feet on the coffee table.

The sun was setting through the french doors, and the swimming pool turned red as blood.

Suddenly I felt something thumping against my foot. The coffee table? I banged on it with my foot. The coffee table

25

banged back. I rapped on it with my knuckles: *da-da-da-dum*, Beethoven's Fifth.

Da-da-da-dum.

I tried *Shave and a Haircut.*

Two bits.

Then the whole coffee table started to sort of rattle and shake. The statuette of Bela Lugosi went crashing to the floor. The velvet tablecloth started to slide down to the carpet. I realized that it wasn't a coffee table at all. It was a coffin.

I didn't have time to scream because the lid flew open, and a man stepped out.

"Oh," he said, "sorry."

He didn't look like Bela Lugosi or Christopher Lee—and he sure didn't look anything like Gary Oldman. He didn't seem as old as any of them. He wasn't wearing a black tux and a cape, either. In fact, all he had on were some purple designer sweats. He looked like any of my friends' fathers, about to go jogging or to the tennis courts.

"Mr. Teppish?" I said.

"Are you dinner?" he said.

"Excuse me?"

He took a long look at me. He noticed the silver ankh around my neck. "You must be one of Rebecca's friends," he said. "I told her to make sure they were marked. Wouldn't want to risk, you know, a little accident. The munchies. Always get the munchies when I wake up."

He put the lid back on the coffin, and carefully replaced the velvet drape, though not the statuette. He put that on the piano, and I saw that there was a dust-free square on the piano lid, where the statuette evidently belonged. "I hate it when she puts things on my coffin," said Mr. Teppish. "By the way, none of this Mr. Teppish crap. You can just call me Vlad."

"Okay, uh, Vlad."

"You . . . ah . . . like my daughter?"

"Well, I hardly know her yet, and—"

"Don't shilly-shally around, boy! You've far less time than you know. Hello is only a moment, but good-bye is forever; do you know how many good-byes can pile up in a thousand years? Two thousand?"

"Well, if you put it that way—yes, I like her."

There! I'd gone and said it. What a foolish, impetuous, adolescent thing to do. I was glad she wasn't around to hear it.

Mr. Teppish sat down at the piano and started playing. I expected something brooding and classical, but actually it was sort of a cocktail lounge medley of pop tunes. I even recognized a Nirvana song. He talked while he played—it's amazing how some people can concentrate on several different things at once like that—now and then stopping to brush off the cobwebs. "It's a problem, you know. The hormones, I mean. I tried to protect her for years, but it's now or never, I suppose. You have to allow them to get hurt sometimes. That's what I hear. One gets out of the childbearing habit after a few millennia, doesn't quite know how to . . . if only I could reach her mother . . . but her coffin is plated with silver, and buried beneath the bed of a stream, and she has a horseshoe clasped to her heart. Oh, oh, what a terrible disaster, that I should be the one left behind to cope with those damnable hormones!"

"Mr. Teppish—Vlad—it's not really that serious! At least, not yet."

"She only has a few days left, Johnny, did you say your name was?"

I didn't remember telling him my name. But this family seemed to be really good at reading minds. I got the old *Twilight Zone* feeling for a moment, before I realized that I had a couple of school books with me, and my name was scrawled in bright red marker on their covers. What a relief.

27

"A few days?" I blurted out. "Why, are you guys leaving town?"

"No . . . it's an identity thing. On her sixteenth birthday, she's going to have to decide. For all time."

"Decide?"

"Her mother, you see, was a mortal."

He stopped playing abruptly, got up and rooted around in a mahogany bar. "Glass of wine? I don't, myself."

"You'll only card me," I said, and he laughed and poured me a warm Coke.

"But I hear Rebecca. I must be off soon. Good luck, young man, and don't break her heart. Eternity is a long time to have a broken heart. There comes a time, you see, when you realize that what's broken will never be mended, never, never at all."

I heard my sister and Rebecca coming back down the corridor, and I was really glad not to be alone with this guy much longer. For a moment, I was starting to buy into the fantasy. *Keep calm*, I told myself. *Keep calm.*

As soon as Astrid entered the room, Mr. Teppish began to act weird. He sniffed the air like a hunting dog, and then he began murmuring: "Blood, blood, there's blood in the room," and looked around, sort of shaking.

"Oh, Daddy, stop it," Rebecca began, and then Astrid let out a little shriek and ran into my arms.

"I knew it, people know, they can just tell, they can smell it on me," she said, and started bawling up a storm. I did what I could to comfort her, but she'd had a trying day, I guess. So I just let her cry until she'd had enough.

Mr. Teppish snapped out of it.

"I suppose I'd better go," he said.

He flung open the french doors and then he sort of got up a running start, and then sprinted out of there—out over the pool deck, over the pool, over the edge of the deck, over the side of the hill and . . .

"Oh, my God! He's committing suicide," said Astrid.

"It's okay," said Rebecca. "Look. There he is." She pointed.

In the twilight, streaking across the splotchy magenta clouds, we saw a raven winging down toward Beverly Hills. It was a beautiful bird, big and powerful and black as the coming night.

I thought for sure that Astrid was going to have a fit. But she just looked calmly out over the city, watched the raven as it swooped, and didn't bat an eye. Like she was hypnotized or something.

Then she said, "You two probably have a lot to talk about. Far be it from me to interrupt you *teenagers*." She kind of glared at Rebecca then, and Rebecca glared back. What had happened between them? "Bye, bro," said Astrid. "I'm off."

And that was the strangest thing of all, because Astrid *never* liked to leave any place early. Her curiosity always got in the way. But before I could say anything, she had gathered her Rollerblades and was whizzing out through the French doors and down the driveway, and Rebecca reached out and held both my hands in hers, and I couldn't think straight for a moment.

"My dad gave you the third degree?" she said.

"Kind of," I said. "But he didn't ask the usual things like, 'What are your goals, young man, do you think you'll be able to give my daughter all the luxuries she deserves?' you know, that kind of thing. It was a lot weirder than that. Stuff about eternity, and identity, and other, you know, abstractions."

"He fusses over nothing."

"But what's this about you having to make some big decision when you turn sixteen?"

"I have to decide who I'm going to be."

"Let me guess. Human or vampire."

29

"But I know what I want," she said, and she kissed me, just a fleeting little kiss, comfortless and cold.

"Your parents . . . are they divorced?"

"Mom's gone," she said. "Consumed, so they say, by her own passion, literally."

I sighed. "Do you want to work on our papers now?" I said.

"You must be joking! You didn't come here for that. . . ."

Of course, that was true, but it didn't mean that I enjoyed having my ulterior motives exposed. "What do you want to do then?" I said. "We could, I don't know . . . go to a movie."

She laughed. "Oh, Johnny, Johnny," she said, "my beautiful cowboy, there's a lot better places to be tonight that the movies . . . come on, Johnny, the night is young. And it's true what my dad says. I don't have much time. Let's go, let's go. . . ."

"I don't have a car," I said.

"There are other ways to travel," she said.

She yanked me by the arm and led me out of the parlor, down a twisty corridor that ended in a spiral staircase. She didn't slow down, but half dragged me up those steps, which seemed to go on and on. . . . In fact, I felt winded; I felt breathless; I felt lightheaded. "What's this, some kind of medieval turret?" I gasped.

"Shut up and keep up," she said.

Landing after landing. The metal steps rattled. At some point, we must have gone through the roof, because I could feel a wind blowing; but my eyes were closed half the time. "Now stop," she said.

I stopped. Opened my eyes.

It was sort of a lookout, with steel railings, and it was the top of some kind of tower that jutted up from the house. It really was windy; at the top of Mulholland Drive, it hardly feels like being in the city because you're above the smog, and now and then there's coyotes and mountain lions. There was a full moon, too, and it made Rebecca's face even more pallid. Her eyes glowed and her hair sort of billowed around her features like a dark halo. We had a lot more in common than just our birthday, I realized. We were both lost.

"I'm only half a vampire," Rebecca said. "About the juice I said I was drinking at lunch? I kind of lied. Well, like, it actually was blood. But I don't have to have blood. Unless I accept the change."

"How many are there like you?" I said. I wanted to play along with her fantasy because it was so, I don't know, so magical, so much better than the real world.

"Not many," she said. "Vampires don't normally reproduce sexually; we have other ways. But sometimes . . . in very special circumstances . . . well, there's love, you see. There's love so powerful it can cross the boundary between the living and the dead. I'm a love child. It's a famous love, too, celebrated in a lot of songs and stuff." She started humming one to me, and I recognized it as an old Timmy Valentine song, "You're Killing Me All Over Again." "Timmy was one of us," she said. "And now he's gone beyond."

Of course, Timmy Valentine's mysterious disappearance happened during my country music days, but even I knew that the reclusive teenage rock star used to give concerts dressed as a vampire, and now that he's vanished from the face of the earth he's become almost as big as Elvis.

"What do you mean, gone beyond?" I asked her.

"There's a place beyond eternity. What eternity is to you, that place is to the immortals. I'd say it's the place all vampires dream of, except that vampires don't dream."

She gripped my arm real tight when she said that. I think she scratched me. She bent down to kiss it better, I think, but when she looked up at me there was a smear of blood on the edge of her lip. It wasn't funny. It was schizophrenia, or something. She needed help.

31

"That support group that Mrs. Chapman talked about," I said. "You still want us to sign up?"

"Support group, yeah, why not," she said. The wind came stronger now. It was howling. L.A.'s not that warm in October, but this wind was totally making my bones feel like icicles. "But now it's time to party."

"What are we doing up here, anyway?" Maybe this was her idea of a good place to, you know, scam. Being cold and all, so you'd have to huddle together for warmth.

"We're waiting for a taxi," she said, and looked out toward the horizon, in the direction of Malibu.

CHAPTER FIVE

CAFÉ
TRANSYLVANIA

She didn't speak for a long time, just looked outward. The clouds were parting, and you could see the lights of the city and the valley stretching out in every direction.

Then I heard a sound above the rushing wind . . . a sound like the beating of great wings. I looked up. Something was swallowing the moon. It didn't get dark, because we were still awash in the glow of the city beneath. Rebecca clasped my hands in hers. "Time to go," she said. Then everything went black. Like someone had thrown a big black cloak over us and whisked us into the sky.

I couldn't see her. I could only hear the screaming wind, and I knew we were flying. I couldn't see where we were going but it had to be fast. *She's pushed me over the ledge!* I thought. We kept accelerating. It was worse than the Batman ride at Magic Mountain. Then, just when I thought we'd about hit terminal velocity, we swerved, corkscrewed, did a stomach-turning three-sixty, then started to slow down. Then I felt her hand in mine . . . like a chunk of ice. When was she ever going to thaw?

"Johnny," she said, "we're almost there."

"What's happening?"

"Relax. Enjoy the ride."

After that, it wasn't so bad. I still couldn't see anything, but the darkness that enveloped us was velvety and smelled faintly of incense. I squeezed Rebecca's hand. Behind the cold, I thought I could sense some residue of warmth. After all, she was only half a vampire. She still had feelings.

Presently the darkness shattered and we found ourselves in an alley. The pieces of the darkness were flapping, chittering, like a flock of crows. Then the fractured blackness kind of merged together and several teenagers materialized. "Thanks for the ride, dudes," Rebecca said. "These are my friends, Johnny. Here's Trace . . . Jeremy . . . Vanina."

Trace was a gangly kid in a black leather jacket. He had a safety pin stuck through his nose. He cackled and waved at me. Jeremy was a short guy, no more than thirteen. He looked like he'd stepped off the set of one of those sitcoms, the ones with lots of perky little kids. Except that his face was as pallid as the others'. Vanina was a girl about Rebecca's age, maybe a little older; but they could almost be twins. Except when Vanina smiled her fangs were totally pointy. "Yo, Johnny," she said. "Sorry you're wearing that amulet."

"Be nice," said Jeremy. "You know Rebecca's not really one of us yet either."

"If you say so," Vanina said. Trace only leered.

We walked down the alley toward some boulevard . . . Sunset I guess it was . . . full of flashing neon and bumper-to-bumper cars. People were just streaming into the comedy clubs at this hour. We didn't cause a stir at all. Plenty of teenagers looking just like this pack were loafing around the streets, some with hungry eyes, some homeless maybe. I lagged behind. I wasn't used to these people, didn't know how to take them. Rebecca stayed close to me.

"Why do they let Jeremy boss them around?" I said.

"He's the oldest."

"What, he got bitten when he was a kid and he's been around for a thousand years?"

"He's almost as old as my dad," Rebecca said. "The others are like, our age, though. Don't be scared. You're wearing the life medallion. No one will hurt you."

"Were we flying or what just now?"

"I don't really understand it myself. It's like a vortex or something. You'd have to ask Jeremy. He's the only one who can do it."

"Hurry," Jeremy snapped.

I started to tell him to lay off, but Rebecca touched my elbow and said, "You'd be sulky too, if you had to look like that for a thousand years. Anyway, we need him. He's the best one at it."

"At what?"

"You'll see."

We turned a corner and there was this building. I could have sworn I would have walked right by it. It wasn't so much a building as a doorway crammed in between a Pizza Hut and a Tower Records. We trooped inside.

"Not many humans get to see this," Rebecca whispered in my ear. "It's Café Transylvania."

To tell you the truth, it wasn't all that impressive. It was smoky. It had a pool table and some beat-up video game machines. It had some dusty old sofas and a counter where some dude was pouring drinks. There were movie posters on the walls—even *The Beast That Threw Up Schenectady*. A bunch of other young people—or vampires, I suppose—were sitting around talking. There was a juke box that was blasting out a Senseless Vultures song.

It reminded me of the rec room at the YMCA back in Wall, South Dakota. Except the kids all wore black. Wasn't exactly my idea of a wild hangout at all.

"This is what you guys do?" I said, sitting down on one of the sofas. A mouse darted out from under the cushion and popped down a hole. The thought of kicking it at the Y for all eternity didn't strike me as being much of a thrill. But maybe there was more to it than met the eye.

Jeremy gave Rebecca one of those "What did you bring *him* for?" kind of looks, and she glared at him defiantly. Then she took my hand and led me up to the counter.

This place might have been called Café Transylvania, but I didn't smell any coffee. I didn't want to make a fool of myself by asking for a double mocha latte or some other yuppie coffeehouse concoction, so I just sat on a barstool and let Rebecca do the ordering. "A bloody Mary for me," she said, "and a virgin Mary for my friend."

Mine tasted like tomato juice. Hers was a little frothier-looking than mine. Both drinks were crimson.

"Is that what I think it is?" I said.

"No alcohol, they'd have to card me for that," she said. "Just a bit of type O. That's the blandest flavor."

"Human?"

She didn't answer me for a while. Then she said, "I'm not a real vampire yet. But I need to get my metabolism, you know, used to the idea. Right now, I have to admit I don't totally like the taste of it. Want a sip?"

I shuddered. You see, I was now getting closer and closer to just taking everything she said literally. Hadn't I seen her father change into a raven? Hadn't I flown on the wings of night? Wasn't I in a dank, dark room surrounded by waiflike kids with china doll complexions and glazed, ruby eyes?

I looked at the glass she held out to me. The liquid seemed almost alive. I felt kind of a tug. The blood called out to me. It echoed in my own veins, made my heart pound faster. Suddenly I *could* see the attraction of it. I was tingling. And I hadn't even tasted the blood, it was just the thought.

Rebecca smiled and said, wistfully, "I wish you were coming with me."

"With me?"

"Into the darkness."

Almost on cue, the jukebox switched to a Timmy Valentine song, the one that goes:

> *Come into my coffin*
> *Don't wanna sleep alone—*

You know it. You've seen the video. It shows an open coffin being lowered into the ground, with Timmy inside, and all these foxy ladies are throwing roses into the grave, the whole video's like, black-and-white except for the roses, big splashes of red . . . and later on in the video it shows the grave all sealed up, and it's snowing, and there's a single red rose by the tombstone, and the inscription reads ALONE ALONE ALONE.

And I said, "Is that why you told me about yourself? Is that why you invited me to your house? So you could take me to the grave?"

"I liked you from the moment I saw you, Johnny," she said softly. "I think I could love you. And you *could* agree to become one of us. In the kingdom of the vampires, the age of consent is sixteen. Well, there's Jeremy, but in the days when *he* became a vampire, there weren't so many rules."

She smiled. She was beautiful. I downed the whole glass of blood, and God, I felt dizzy and woozy and trembly and all-powerful, felt all those things at the same time. Everything was spinning except Rebecca's face, and that smile. . . . Her lips smiled but her eyes were blank, like pieces of colored glass . . . and she leaned forward and kissed me.

"Do you think you could love me too? Just a little? A tiny

morsel of love that will nourish me through the centuries of gloom?"

I wanted to say yes, wanted to shout it out. The whole room was whirling around me. I would have agreed to anything. Maybe it was just the hormones, but it was the most powerful feeling in the world.

Then I heard Vanina shrieking; "Time, guys, time to go hunting!"

"Come on!" Rebecca shouted, and grabbed my hand. "Surf's up!"

Surf? What were they talking about? But the lethargy I'd sensed when I first walked into this place was gone. The young vampires were all charged up. They were silent, listening for something I couldn't hear . . . some hidden music in the night air. Jeremy was concentrating hardest of all. At last, he said, "East of here. Where Cherokee crosses Sunset." And all at once everyone was dashing for the exit.

"Hold on to me!" Rebecca said. "Or they'll be gone!"

I ran. But running wasn't enough. We were in the alley in a moment, then we all turned . . . a dark whirlwind, rushing uphill along Sunset. The streets were dead. We were a pack of wolves . . . we were the darkness itself . . . a speeding void . . . the whistling of the chill air. I can't explain it. I was still human, still me, and yet I was part of them, too. I had only felt this way in dreams before. Maybe that's all this was.

Once more the darkness shattered and we found ourselves in another alley. We were behind some apartments. A Dumpster stood against a wall, and there was a hut made from old pizza boxes leaning against it. Rival crews had tagged the Dumpster till you couldn't see past the graffiti.

A man was lying by the hut . . . a homeless man. Unshaven, dirty . . . the kind of person they kept out of Encino so the rich wouldn't have to look at them. Jeremy knelt down beside him and whispered into his ear. "Wake up, pal. Your

sand is running out." And poked him gently in the ribs. Play-
fully. Like you play with your food. The man woke up.
Looked into Jeremy's eyes. I don't know what he saw exactly,
but he started screaming. I was scared and horrified but I
couldn't look away. The man got to his feet and started to
run. And the whole pack followed. Up the alley where there
was a dead end. He turned. We stood there, a dozen or so
of us. He turned back, tried to scale the wall, but was too
weak from malnutrition, I guess. Or maybe he just knew his
number was up, and he didn't want to fight it anymore.

The vampires pounced. At last, I averted my eyes. I heard
slurping sounds. I staggered over to the Dumpster and
threw up.

I don't know how long I was doubled up beside the pizza
box dwelling. At last I felt Rebecca's hand on my shoulder.
"It's not so bad," she said softly.

She took my hand in hers. And this was the strangest
thing: Her hands had been freezing cold all evening, but now
they were warm, human.

"I hate the taste of heroin," Vanina was complaining.
"Next time let's not have Jeremy pick it out. He's a sicko,
always goes for the tainted blood."

"It's just because he's old," Trace said. "They get jaded,
they want a little more flavor. One day it'll get so *nothing*
can get his tastebuds going."

"There's always HIV," Vanina said. "But that's too spicy
for me."

"They're talking about him like he's not even the same
species," I said. "They just murdered him, for crying out
loud."

Rebecca said, "When you eat a hamburger, do you think
about how you murdered the cow?"

"But they chased him! There was nothing humane about
the way they—"

40

"Adrenalin improves the flavor," said Rebecca. "Had enough for the night?"

"Yeah," I said. "But I don't have a ride home."

"I've got money," she said. "We'll take a taxi."

We didn't speak the whole way back to Encino. I walked her to her front door. I didn't kiss her good night or anything. I was still feeling sick to my stomach. I turned away and started walking back down the driveway, and she said, "Think about it, Johnny. Think about that Timmy Valentine song. You know the one I mean."

I stopped to look at her. She was still beautiful, still vulnerable. I remembered that electric surge that had overwhelmed me at the taste of blood. I hated myself for it, but I knew that the thrill of it was real. Blood was power.

I was angry at myself for watching them kill that homeless dude, and not doing anything about it, and then barfing on top of it all. What could I have done, called 911, told them a flock of vampires was cruising down Sunset? It wasn't what I'd seen and heard and tasted that night that made me mad. It was the fact that I'd seen something unspeakably evil, and yet I wasn't as totally horrified as I should have been. I'd seen something else, too. They were monsters, these kids, but they had something I didn't have. They belonged to each other. There was a sense of communion there, of family.

And that's the thing that tempted me the most.

CHAPTER SIX

Astrid's Warning

Astrid was waiting up for me. And that was the oddest thing of all, because it was way, way past her bedtime, and it wasn't like her to worry about me.

She was half-asleep on the sofa, the lights were still on, and a Humphrey Bogart movie was on the television. When I closed the front door, she came to right away. "Are you all right?"

"What are you doing? Why aren't you in bed?"

"Oh, nothing. I wanted to watch *The Maltese Falcon*."

"Yeah, right. It's not as if you don't have cable in your own room."

"Okay," she said. "The truth." She looked at me, all serious now. "There's something really wrong with that girl. You've got to be careful, Johnny."

It's always annoying when your little sister starts meddling in your affairs, so I wasn't too pleased. Then she said, "It was a good idea for you to get me to talk to an older girl, but . . . well . . . Rebecca didn't know anything about

S. P. Somtow

the subject. It's never happened to her." Astrid was very
smug and superior about it all.

"But—"

"She says it's genetic—parts of her development are de-
layed until her big decision day—so it seems I'm more of a
woman than her. Oh, we took care of my problem okay.
She's got an Internet link in her bedroom—we just logged
on and rooted around in 'alt.adolescent.angst.FAQ'."

I had to admit that I had no idea what she was talking
about. Sometimes she gets this way when she's with Mikey,
the sixth grader with the monstrous computer across the
street. I said, "So she's a late developer. I don't see why
you're waiting up for me and offering all these dire
warnings."

"It's worse than you think! I went over to Mikey's after-
ward—"

"But he goes to bed at eight!"

"I know, but I climbed in his window."

"You what! Wait till everyone down in James Dean Ele-
mentary finds out that the hottest girl in the sixth grade
went climbing in the window of that geek!"

"Hey," she said primly, "at least he has a mind. Besides,
Romeo and Juliet were only seventh graders, and no one
bitches about them."

"Okay," I said. I went to the kitchen for a glass of milk.
Something to wash down the lingering taste of blood and
vomit. I fetched her some too, then found a half-eaten bag
of soft cookies in the cupboard. I sat down next to her on
the sofa and put my arm around her, and she kind of purred
as she chowed down on the cookies. "So what hideous facts
did you discover at Mikey's?"

"Okay. I looked up Tepes in his database." She picked up
a wad of papers that had been lying on the floor. "You might
want to look through this stuff. Do you know *who* Vlad
Tepes is, or was?"

44

"Does it matter?"

"Dracula," said my sister, and thrust the papers into my arms. "All in all," she added, "Mikey may be a dweeb, but I think my love life is probably a heck of a lot more healthy than yours."

I hate mouthy twelve-year-olds.

So, I took the papers up to my room. Put them down on the desk. Then I put one of my fancy dancing trophies on top of it. I got into bed; after all, it was a school night.

As soon as I closed my eyes, I had a dream about fancy dancing, which was a strange thing because I'd turned my back on all that Indian stuff. But there I was, in a dream, doing it . . . high summer in South Dakota somewhere, just me in the sunlight, left toes left heel right toes right heel left toes left heel right toes right heel then caper, up, up, and the anklets jangling jangling jangling and I don't know where the drums are coming from but the voice that wails above them is my *tunkashila's*. I'm all in white, white feathers, white leggings, white paint. I'm dancing, but it's not a competition or anything like that, I'm just dancing. Then a huge dark cloak gets thrown over the sun and there's someone else dancing too, but his feathers are raven feathers and his face is all withered and his eyes are crimson as fresh blood. The drumbeats accelerate. I leap! I can fly! I'm hanging in the air! There's a great wind billowing across the prairie and I feel free and full of strength. And then I see that the raven is leaping farther, flying higher, soaring and swooping over the silver-black clouds. And all of a sudden I'm losing all my confidence and I start to fall. And the raven sees me plummet and sweeps downward, his wings wide open, his fangs glittering . . . and there is no sun anymore, never will be, the sunlight is gone forever. . . .

*   *   *

45

I woke up. It was, I don't know, some time in the wee hours. The house was deathly still. I snapped on the bedside lamp, took down Astrid's sheaf of papers, and started to read.

Vlad Tepes—a historical figure, more than five hundred years ago—ruler of a rock-girt principality called Transylvania. Known as Dracula—sort of a nickname. Known as the Impaler—which is what he dearly loved to do. Impaling, in this case, usually meant shoving a stake . . . well, like, it wasn't through the heart. It took a totally long time to die.

Bram Stoker borrowed the name when he came to write this book, *Dracula,* the book that made vampire a household word, a hundred years ago. Probably got the idea for the stake through the heart, too.

Hardly the man who sat around the house in sweats, told me to call him "Vlad," and was agonizing about his daughter's identity crisis . . . or was he? Or at least some kind of descendant?

But the real Vlad had never been a vampire. Bram Stoker made that up. I mean, it was only a novel. Or was it?

I went on reading. The things Vlad used to do were pretty sickening by today's standards, but some people weren't too displeased about it. I read that some Romanians regard him as a national hero. He himself did all that impaling in the name of Christianity. One time he impaled thousands of people and had a big dinner party surrounded by his victims dying on stakes. What a fun-loving dude.

By the time I finished reading, it was dawn. I didn't feel like going back to sleep, so I went down to the kitchen and fixed myself a bowl of cereal.

There was a tap on the kitchen door. . . .

She stood there, framed by the K-Mart chintz curtains, slender and fragile in the morning light. She was even more beautiful than last night. Her skin had this translucent shine to it. Maybe it was just the dawn and seeing her through the freshly Windexed windows. I had read all that stuff and I'd had that nightmare, which had to be significant . . . but there she was. What could I say?

"Let me in," she said. "I have to be invited, you know."

"No you don't," I said, "not until you're a full-fledged vampire." I opened the door. "How do you manage to look so refreshed?"

"Right now," she said, "I'm able to switch back and forth, you know, like being a dual national and having two passports. I can wake up as if I've had a full night's sleep because . . . when I'm out there doing vampire stuff . . . it's almost like I've been dreaming."

"Don't you wish you could be on the borderline forever? You'd never have to sleep at all."

"But where would I belong?" she said, with a deep melancholy.

"I can really relate to that," I said.

"I know," she said. "Get your Rollerblades, I want to show you something."

Unsteadily—I'd barely had any sleep, remember—I followed Rebecca Teppish down the hill. Just before we hit Ventura Boulevard, she made a sharp left down a tiny street I don't think I'd ever noticed before. It wasn't even paved, and it ran between the back of an apartment complex and a high stucco wall that was covered with gangsters' taggings. The graffiti was all in black and red and I saw that some of Rebecca's friends' writings were up there . . . Trace and Vanina, that is . . . Trace's in hard, angular strokes, Vanina's in elegant, twisty curlicues.

Rollerblading was difficult here; it was all uphill and the dirt path was all rocky. But at last we reached a wrought iron gate, and she waved at me to stop. She pushed at the gate. It wasn't oiled, and the creak almost tore my ears off. A sign read:

Star Haven

and beneath it were the words:

Eternal Rest

But the sign wasn't on straight, and it swayed in the breeze. I don't mind cemeteries; to me they are peaceful places. I'm not really scared of dead people. In South Dakota my grandfather used to take me to Wounded Knee every couple of months so that I could talk to my great-grandfather.

I never thought that my great-grandfather said anything, but *Tunkashila* heard plenty. But then again, he is almost a *wichasha wakan,* a medicine man. Certainly he's enough of one to trick thousands of yuppie New Agers into buying his book of ancient wisdom!

This cemetery wasn't like any other one I'd been to—not Forest Lawn where the stars are buried in their cars and in fake Mayan temples and stuff like that—not the Jewish cemetery on Melrose and what, Cahuenga? where my mom's dad lies. It was all overrun with weeds, so you could hardly see any headstones or monuments.

"Don't worry," she said. "It's not consecrated ground or anything like that. This burial ground is owned by a friend." Not that that would bother *me,* but I guess it was something she always had to worry about.

We heard a movement.

"Quiet," she said. "Behind this tree for a moment."

Almost completely obscured by oleander bushes was some kind of monument with a low iron railing around it. There were people in front of it. They were laying wreaths and lighting candles. It was a man and a woman. They were real old, maybe as old as my tunkashila. They prayed—or whatever it is people do at gravesites, meditated, reflected, whatever—for a long while, and then they sort of slunk away, almost as though they had no right to be there.

"Come on," she said when they had left.

We scrambled over vines and reached the monument.

"Just look at that!" she said. She was very agitated. She started to climb the rail—the little gate was locked—and was furiously kicking the flower wreaths out of the way.

"What's wrong? It looks nice."

"Wrong? Did you get a look at that?"

She picked something up off the ground. It was a garlic bulb.

"They know," she said. "They've known for months. If someone didn't come here every week and clear away the garlic, they'd never be able to get out."

"Who?"

She pulled up a whole strand of garlic, the kind you see hanging on the wall in Italian restaurants. When she had brushed all the flowers out of the way, I saw the inscription, on a marble stele set into the ground:

$$\text{Tracy and Vanina}$$
$$\text{1970—1985}$$
$$\text{Together in Life and Death}$$

and I said, "But that was—"

But before I could finish, Rebecca said, "That's right. They never saw the nineties. Sad, huh?"

Behind the stele was the monument itself, one of those overblown things that rich people have, with Greek columns, a statue of an angel, you know, all that pretentious garbage. There was a doorway, too, with steps leading downward. . . .

"We have to go in," Rebecca said. "They may have tried to sabotage the crypt."

I followed her down the steps. It wasn't like in horror movies. It was all clean. The crypt was all marble. Rebecca switched on the light. It was fluroescent lighting, flat and cold. Two big old stone coffins stood in the center of the crypt and yes, Rebecca was right: there were wreaths of garlic all over them, and around the two sarcophagi was a circle of silver dollars.

"Why didn't they just stake them?" I said.

"Have a heart," Rebecca said. "Would you be able to pound a stake though the heart of your own kid?"

I shut up. Helped Rebecca pick up all the silver coins and gather the garlic to throw away outside. I knew a guy who collected silver dollars, maybe I could sell them to him. Was that stealing? I thought. Were Vanina and Trace really in there, resting in their native earth, waiting for nightfall so that they could run down another homeless dude and suck him dry? Whose side was I on, anyway?

"It's almost time for school," I said at last.

"Yeah."

Fifteen minutes later we stood at the entrance to Claudette Colbert High, and we heard a bell ringing, and she suddenly turned to me and said, "Do you know what I wish, more than anything in the world?"

"What?" I said.

"To do normal, human things. Go to a movie. Go to parties. Fall in love. That most of all. With you, if you'll have me."

"If I'll have you!" I said. "You're only the most exotic, beautiful, intriguing, amazing, maddening girl I've ever met in my whole life—"

"I want to do those things and I only have a few days left to do them in before I have to go into the dark places forever—"

"You make it sound like you're becoming a nun, or something."

She laughed bitterly.

I said, "But the truth is, you don't have to be a vampire at all, do you? You could rebel. You could fight it. You don't have to squeeze all that's human into a few more days—"

We went inside the school and down to our lockers. Other people in our class were calling out, "Yo, Johnny," or "Hi, Rebecca," but we didn't pay any attention to them.

"You could have a whole lifetime," I said.

"Only one lifetime?"

And she began to cry, I mean *really* cry, the kind of crying you do when someone dies. What could I do? I had to take her in my arms. I had to kiss away her tears and try to give her cold flesh some of my warmth.

I didn't care that it was in front of the whole school, and that the news that we were now an item would be common knowledge by lunch.

CHAPTER SEVEN

EXTRAORDINARY THINGS

Deciding to do ordinary things was easy enough, but there are so many ordinary things in the world. And ordinary things can be pretty extraordinary if you are doing them for the first and last and only time.

Rebecca had never gone bowling. She'd never ridden the rollercoasters at Magic Mountain, never been to Disneyland, never even been to a drive-in. There's only one drive-in left in the Valley anyway, but even so, going to the drive-in was part of my growing up, what with having no money and getting in cheaper by the carload. In Mrs. Chapman's class, we sat there next to each other while the other kids gossiped about us, and we didn't speak to each other at all, while Mrs. Chapman hectored us about love and death and all those things that people who are big time into culture like to go on and on about.

In fact, Mrs. Chapman started reading a poem to us. It was called, "To His Coy Mistress," and it was by some ancient dude named Andrew Marvell. Mostly I didn't get much of it—it talked about "vegetable love," which sounded like one of those Santa Monica vegetarian restaurants—but there was one part that made me snap out of my daydream for a moment:

> *The grave's a fine and private place,*
> *But none, I think, do there embrace.*

Okay, so I looked over at Rebecca and she looked at me, and I know we both felt it—that sense of desperation—that feeling that the world was being flushed down the toilet while we stood there doing nothing.

So around lunch I suddenly said, "C'mon, let's ditch," and she nodded, and I knew she'd been thinking the same thing all morning.

We slipped off campus, took another of those little streets that wind up and down the Santa Monica Mountains, and we ended up at my house. I went in on tiptoe, but I heard my grandfather calling me from the garage. I guess you just can't sneak by him.

"It's okay, Rebecca," I said. "He's cool."

We went through the den into the garage. My grandpa was sitting in his usual position. Today he was more traditional than usual, shirtless and wearing deerskin breeches and an eagle feather in his hair. Rebecca was a little in awe of him. People are always amazed at the two sundance scars on his chest, little white worms on his tanned, weathered skin. I think he must have been psyching himself up for his big signing at the Beverly Center, although I wasn't at all sure that he was going to say anything at it since I made him mad at me that day.

"*Hau,*" he said amiably. "Ditching, I suppose."

"*Tunkashila,* this is Rebecca Teppish."

"Oh yes," he said, "the *winchinchala* who isn't quite human. Sit down, sit down."

He didn't offer her any tobacco because that's a man's thing, and he's not very nineties when it comes to the gender role thing; Mrs. Chapman would have had a hard time with him.

Then, to me, he said something that startled the hell out of me. "The raven is dancing at your back. Don't think he can outleap you. You must race him clear into the sunrise."

"*Tunkashila*—my dream—" I said.

"Don't look at me," Rebecca said. "I never dream."

"Ah, but you should see him dance," said Grandpa. "You know, there's a powwow this coming Friday . . . the last big one before it gets too cold to dance outside. I'm planning to go. Get ready for this latest foolery those publishers want me to do. Why don't you come, Johnny? Bring the *winchinchala*. Show her a good time, before that bad old raven snatches her away." My heart sank when Grandpa talked about dancing, because I could pretty much predict which way the conversation was going to go now . . . and it did.

"Dance?" Rebecca said. "I never knew you could dance. Oh, show me. We could dance together. Is it Indian dancing?"

Grandpa rolled his eyes.

"Oh, dear," Rebecca said. "Did I do something politically incorrect?"

Grandpa stared into her eyes, and then started to laugh. "There is a twinge of human being inside her," he said to me. "You could nurture it if you wanted to. Or kill it."

Rebecca wanted to change the subject I guess, so she started badgering me about dancing again. Then Grandpa started singing a song that you sing when you're sort of gently taunting a dancer who's standing around in street clothes and won't dance. It goes like this:

Wachi wichasha toka cha niglutan shni hwo?
* *Dancer, what's wrong, why aren't you dressed for dancing?*

And Rebecca started clapping the rhythm. That song has a kind of aggravating quality to it, it kind of grabs hold of your feet and pretty soon you can't help it and start to go right toes right heel left toes left heel and on and on and then you start jumping around and whooping. And Rebecca got caught up in that rhythm too and she got up and started doing it, which kind of upset my *tunkashila* a bit because actually, the women are supposed to move slowly around in a circle, and not leap about. These days of course, they do leap, but well, that was my grandpa. And of course he was too tolerant to say she couldn't leap. Lakota don't tell people what to do; they're total individualists.

So we leaped and he sang until we were exhausted, and then Astrid came home from school. She wasn't too happy to see Rebecca, but then the two girls went into the kitchen and made tuna fish sandwiches—something Rebecca had never done before—and we ate. That, too, was such an ordinary thing, but maybe to Rebecca it partook of the same quality that last night had had for me.

"You've never made a sandwich?" Astrid was saying in astonishment, though I'm not sure she thought it was on a par with never having had her period.

"Sometimes I don't even eat for days," said Rebecca.

"You do look a smidgin anorexic."

"She doesn't always need solid food," I said.

"Yeah, right, her metabolism," Astrid said. "Fluctuating. Not one thing, not the other."

Rebecca took another bite. "Very exotic," she said. "Very, I don't know, intoxicating almost, this ordinary people kind of stuff."

The phone rang; it was the school's computer, which automatically calls your house if you ditch. But Grandpa told them it was a family medical emergency. "We're trying to prevent my grandson from turning into a raven," he said to the school computer's sound digitizer. "We'll give you a full update on his progress."

I wondered what the office would make of it—not to mention the fact that it was true.

"What will your father tell them?" I asked Rebecca.

"He's really out of it in the daytime," she said.

Astrid and Rebecca glared at each other and I realized there was a little more than just concern for me in Astrid's attempts to sabotage my relationship with Rebecca. There was a certain amount of jealousy, too. Astrid didn't want to share her big brother with anyone.

In fact, when I suggested that Rebecca and I go to the drive-in that night, she immediately said, "Yes, but you don't have a car. Who's going to take you—the Count?"

"Well," I said, "with Mom in Mexico, and the keys in the flowerpot—"

"No you don't," said Astrid, "or I'm telling."

"Okay, so you think of something."

"Well, Mikey's mom said she would take him and me to a movie if someone older would watch us. She has to go to some computer nerds user meet that's a block away from the drive-in."

"That sucks," I said. "We don't want precocious little geeks underfoot, and anyway you're only saying this because you want to spy on us."

"Take it or leave it."

Rebecca started to laugh. "Nothing could be more ordinary than an evening of sibling rivalry," she said wistfully. "You know, I've never had siblings, and I never will."

"I was hoping for something a little more, you know, romantic," I said. But Rebecca was intent on the ordinary, and I could see that she was trying to win over my sister, too.

At that point, the mail came. It always comes real late in our neighborhood because the mail carriers have to so much ground to cover. There was something addressed to me. The letter was on expensive, creamy paper, and it had a black border around it, like a funeral announcement.

It said:

Dr. Vladimir X. Teppish III
Voivode of the Western Kindred
requests the honor of your company
at the devivification ceremony of his daughter
Rebecca
on All-Hallows' Eve
at Midnight
11899 Tirgoviste Lane, Encino, California
regrets only
evening dress optional
mortal guests are requested to wear silver insignia to avoid
being mistaken for light refreshments

If this was a joke, someone had gone all out. "Devivification ceremony!" I said. "That sounds pretty dire."

"It's sort of like a bat mitzvah for vampires," Rebecca said.

"Bat mitzvah!" Astrid said. "Don't believe a word she says, Johnny. Anyone with even a smattering of Latin can figure out that 'devivification' is just a fancy word for murder! They're gonna kill her, Johnny . . . probably some kind of weird human sacrifice thing . . . probably drink her blood to boot."

"Well, of *course* they're going to kill me," Rebecca said. "How else am I going to become a vampire?"

Mikey and his mom came over shortly after that, and we went off to the drive-in.

Mikey isn't so bad. He doesn't have the appearance of someone who is fixated on computers—he is pretty much a Valley dude skater type—but when he talks, it's all about microprocessors. His mother is the real estate czarina of our block, and she drives around in one of those humongous Cadillacs, which makes some of the other people on our block turn up their noses at here. But it was a big comfortable vehicle to watch movies out of, better than that ancient Caprice we all used to bundle up inside of back in Wall.

The drive-in was showing a double bill of antediluvian movies, a Western and a horror movie, but, as Astrid pointed out, who watches the movie anyway?

Astrid and Mikey certainly didn't. They were out of the car after five minutes, because the drive-in had a video game arcade, bowling alley, pseudo-fifties malt shop, mini-golf course, batting cages, and virtual reality room attached to it. It was sort of a kids' version of paradise.

Pretty soon, I wanted to leave the car, too, because it was one of those cavalry versus Indians kind of Westerns that always makes me feel queasy because I never know who to root for. I pretended I had to go to the bathroom, but I instead, I sat around sipping a vanilla Coke and getting more and more depressed. Now and then I could see my sister and her friend running around being hyper, and I wished I could be that young again. It sure sucked to be almost sixteen and bursting with hormones.

After a while, Rebecca came and joined me. "I'm sorry," I said.

"About what?" she said.

"That this is such a boring evening."

"But it's not," she said. "It's great." She tried my vanilla Coke and smiled. "What is it?"

"You've never had a vanilla Coke?"

"Well, why is that so strange? You never tried a type O cocktail until last night."

"That's different . . ." But was it? Sitting here with her, it was easy to believe that she and I were just sharing our different cultural heritages and learning about different lifestyles . . . just the sort of thing Mrs. Chapman would want her students to be doing.

For the next hour, we didn't go back to the car. We lazed in the coffee shop talking about inconsequential things. Then we played a couple of rounds of miniature golf. We played a few video games. She had lightning reflexes and when she played her eyes went all dead, like she was a soulless machine; she had a way of being able to shut off her emotions, I guess.

Then we got more vanilla Cokes and talked some more. Her childhood in Romania, her father getting the two of them shipped out of the country in coffins, just one step ahead of the Ceausescu secret police. Her mother was an American diplomat; that's how her dad had managed to get his green card. But she was dead now.

"Consumed with passion," Rebecca said. "She'd have made a great vampire. She knew more about vampires than any vampire I've ever met—the history, the traditions, the ancient rituals—but she just couldn't take the crossing."

"That's what you call it? When you step over the boundary between life and death?"

"Yeah. After the ritual draining, an elder of the tribe calls your name . . . calls you forth from the shadowland between death and undeath. You have to hear the call. You have to have it in you. Even before you're a vampire, you have to hear the music of the night. Or you can't make the crossing. You're lost forever. I guess that happened to Mom."

"How do you know that you can—"

"Of course I know, Johnny. I'm halfway there already. And you can too. I know it. You hear the music of the night. When you drank that bloody cocktail, it sang to you. I can tell, Johnny. You're the first person I've ever loved. I feel it."

Pretty heavy stuff. I believed her, too. I'd felt that pounding of the heart, that tingling in the veins. And I had had other inklings too. That dream of the dancer and the raven.

I knew now that that was the kind of dream that my *tunka-shila* called "a sending from the spirit world." I didn't want to agree with Rebecca, but I knew that she could tell what I was thinking.

After a while, she said, "I guess we should go back to the movie."

When we got back, the horror movie was in full swing. It was one of those Z-grade movies, but it did have special effects by Beau Maguire, the "king of splatter," whose kid goes to our school. As we climbed into the backseat—Mikey and Astrid were still nowhere in sight—a young woman was fleeing down a city street. It all looked kind of familiar . . . the neon, the alleys, the homeless man pushing a shopping cart past a stand-up comedy theater . . . and then I remembered the name of the movie: *Dracula in Burbank*. Pretty cheesy. The vampire soon came onto the scene, and it looked as if he was wearing a beat-up Dracula cape left over from some high-budget vampire flick—they have boutiques in Hollywood that sell costumes left over from movie sets, it's easy to pick out something for Halloween there—and he had a pretty cheesy makeup job too. He was chasing the attractive young woman, and she was panting heavily in that way that all B-movie scream queens are so good at, and why so many teenage guys like to watch them. She ran down a deserted alley. Past a Dumpster. Kind of a déjà vu about it all.

Rebecca squeezed my hand. I wondered if she felt the same way I did when I watched Westerns.

"It's almost like one of us *made* this movie," she said. "It's so close to the real thing, only fake."

"Maybe all the studio heads are really vampires," I said.

"Or just the low-budget ones."

"You don't mind them, you know, showing your people in such a negative light?"

She laughed again, a bitter laugh this time. "What, you

think I should call the national vampire antidefamation task force?"

"I think I read about that in the tabloids."

"The thing is, it really exists. Just because you die doesn't mean you get any brighter. There's an element among us that loves to taunt the mortals, that's always dropping clues about our existence to tantalize them . . . I guess I'm like that, too, huh. I mean, blurting it right out in class on my first day of school."

"You knew no one would believe you."

The vampire had the woman cornered. He bared his fangs. Rebecca laughed nervously.

The vampire pounced. The scream queen screamed, and so did Rebecca. I held here tight, but she wriggled free. "I'm not screaming about the movie," she told me. "It's something else. Look."

Three shadows flitted across the movie screen.

I got out of the car and so did Rebecca. I heard someone muttering: "It's those damn bats again." A dude in an orange suit, maybe the manager, was stalking through the lot with a rifle in his hand. "Don't panic, folks," he said to me and Rebecca. "We'll get rid of those pesky creatures."

"Come on," she said, "quick. They're already mad at you for taking up so much of my time. Do you still have that amulet?"

I hadn't taken it off since that night.

"Good," she said. "But they followed us here. They want to hurt us. You, in particular. Or anyone that's close to you."

"Astrid?" I cried in alarm.

Where were those brats?

CHAPTER EIGHT

A CHASE SCENE

She was sitting at the counter in the fake fifties malt shop, gulping down an overpriced black-and-white shake. And Trace and Vanina were looming over her on either side. I breathed a sigh of relief when I saw that she was wearing the amulet. I guess I shouldn't have worried about Astrid; she'd been paranoid about it since she'd downloaded all that data on Vlad the Impaler off the Internet.

Rebecca zeroed in on the three of them. "Don't you dare," she shouted at the two vampires. Trace and Vanina swiveled around in eerie unison.

"Dare?" Vanina said. "Like, she's a charmer. Wouldn't dream of snuffing her. Not without her permission."

Astrid turned to me. "I guess they're okay," she said. She stared straight ahead, not meeting my eyes. Maybe they'd cast some kind of spell on her. She didn't seem all hypered up over the vampire thing like she had before. "They're not going to touch me because I've got the ankh. They said so."

Trace said, "You think we're jealous or something, don't you, Becky."

"You don't realize how long eternity is, yet," said Vanina.

"Enjoy your little Indian boy while you can," said Trace.

"You'll be with us soon. You'll be taking the long view. You'll be saying the first of many good-byes," said Vanina. "And there are so many, right, Trace?"

"Totally," said Trace.

"Thanks for saving us from our parents' garlic fever, by the way," Vanina said to me. "You didn't have to. We like you. No need to put you to sleep at all."

They were treating me like Lassie. That really made me mad, but I didn't want it to show.

"Don't try to hide your anger," Trace said. "Dude, we can smell anger at five hundred paces."

"Our senses are a lot keener than yours. We're part wild animal, you know. We have sonar, like bats, and we can sniff out all your emotions, like dogs, and we can see the aura that clings to you, all the way into the ultraviolet . . . like bees. We are total superbeings. But hey, like, we're your friends, so it's casual."

"They mean it," Rebecca said. "But what about Jeremy?"

"We can't speak for Jeremy," Vanina said. "You know how it is."

"She means that Jeremy was made into a vampire long before we became civilized, and started following the vampire law," Rebecca said. "His identity was only half-formed. Sometimes he's an angry child, trapped inside that three-thousand-year-old intellect, sometimes he just does whatever he feels like—"

"Where's Mikey?" Astrid cried out, abruptly snapping out of whatever they'd done to calm her down.

That's when we saw him. Through the window, behind the bar, dodging in and out of the parked cars. And something else, too. A shadowy blob that oozed across the pavement. Sometimes it seemed to have wings, sometimes paws. And now Mikey was banging on the window of a big old Chevy. Trying to get someone to let him in. He was terrified, and the occupants of the Chevy were all nervous, maybe wondering if they should call the manager or something.

We dashed out of the malt shop. The waiter called, "Hey, you ain't paid yet," and I just said, "We'll be back," as I ran outside.

"We'll stall Jeremy," Trace and Vanina said at the same time.

They casually turned into black cats and sprang into action. I didn't have time to admire their morphing. They zipped over to where Mikey was cowering and they circled him, yowling. That manager with his rifle was coming at them now, shouting, "This isn't a zoo, you know!" and firing a warning shot into the air. It being L.A., everyone went on watching the movie. People mind their own business around here.

I got to the Cadillac. The keys were in it.

"I hate to say this, guys," I said, "but I don't have my license yet. Can you drive it, Rebecca?"

"I can't drive."

"Oh, no," I said. "If I get caught driving without a license, they'll make me wait till I'm eighteen!"

Astrid just stared at us incredulously. "All right," she said. "For crying out loud. *I'll* drive."

She elbowed me to move over, then started backing out.

"I'm too short to see much past the dash," she said. "Scream if we're about to hit something."

She hit something.

"No big deal, just one of those long concrete thingies that help you park straight," she said, and spun out, burning rubber in the process. "Wahoo!" she said.

"Have you ever driven before?" said Rebecca.

"No," she said, "but I have a pretty good theoretical knowledge of how this works—I once checked out the DMV's home page on Mikey's computer." The windshield wipers came on. "Whoops."

She managed to steer over to where Mikey was. She popped the locks. "Get in!" she screamed. He jumped in. Then she peeled out again, screeched past the arcade and the malt shop, knocked over a garbage can, and hit the main boulevard.

Then she ran a red light. Two cars crashed into each other behind us.

"Sorry," she said, "but you should have yelled 'Stop!'"

"Stop!" we shrieked, as another red light came up.

She didn't stop. A couple more cars swerved, lurched into mailboxes, and smashed into the window of an all-night deli.

"I can't seem to reach the brakes," she said, shrugging. "Help me get the seat moved forward."

Mikey said, "This is cool. Don't worry about the Cadillac. Mom says we can get more money from the insurance if we like, totally total it, than if we just scrape it a little."

Then I saw something in the side mirror that made my hair stand on end.

A big, black, wolf was chasing us down the street. A wolf with slavering canines and hard, glittering eyes . . . bigger than any wolf I'd ever seen in the wild . . . faster, too. He was keeping up with us. Could overtake us at any moment, I was sure, because it wasn't any timber wolf.

It had to be Jeremy.

Clunk! He sprang onto the trunk! You could see his eyes reflected in the windshield! Astrid screamed.

Mikey, undaunted, turned around to look at the wolf, who was banging at the rear window with his paws. "He has to be invited," he said. "He can't just come in."

"Don't be too sure of that," said Rebecca. "The rules will only hold Jeremy so far. He's very old, very powerful."

Now Mikey was scared. He's one of those kids that turns

into a chatterbox when he's nervous, and he started blabbing away in his weasly little voice. "But like," he said, "I thought he was so cool, and we were just kicking it and he told me he was a vampire and all, but like, he looked like he was in the sixth grade. We talked about role-playing games. He said he played all of them except the vampire ones, they're a little too much like reality for him, and—"

Thud. The wolf was on the sunroof of the Cadillac. It was tapping at the glass with its paws. You could hear it howling.

Mikey just went on and on. "Anyway like, I don't believe in vampires, I'm way past that fantasizing stage, you know, I'm like, totally advanced in my cognitive development and like, my analyst thinks I should relax more and get back into kid stuff, maybe even regress a bit. So like this kid, he tells me his name's Jeremy Weiss, sounds perfectly innocuous, we talk about hacking for a while and then he's all, 'I don't bother to hack. I just make myself one with the electron stream and dive into cyberspace and go wherever I want,' and I think, either he has a screw loose or he's been reading too many William Gibson novels. So *then* he tells me he's a vampire and—"

"Mikey," said a voice from the sunroof.

Mikey just froze up.

Astrid said, "Oh, my God. I think he's reaching into Mikey's mind, pulling out his thoughts . . . that voice belongs to Mikey's dad."

I looked up. The wolf was gone. Instead, there was a man's face peering down in the moonlight. Mikey's dad was an actor. He had died last year in a car crash.

"Dad . . ." Mikey said.

"Push the button," said the voice. "Open the sunroof. Let me in, Mikey, it's cold up here."

Mikey started to clamber over the seat. "It's not your father!" I screamed.

Astrid started to swerve. She was trying to throw Jeremy off the roof.

"Mikey—Mikey—" said the Jeremy-thing. "Why won't you let me in?"

"Daddy—" Mikey said, sounding more and more like a little boy.

Astrid wove across two lanes, dodged an oncoming truck and suddenly found herself barreling up the on-ramp to the freeway. As Astrid pushed the accelerator all the way down, her head slowly sank below the edge of the steering wheel.

Rebecca screamed.

Astrid passed a Porsche on the right. I saw the driver's jaw drop. It must have looked like no one was driving the Cadillac at all. Astrid showed no sign of slowing down.

Jeremy kept hammering on the sunroof.

Astrid spun the steering wheel hard left, and jackknifed across several more lanes of traffic. Tires were squealing all around us. Jeremy rolled off the sunroof onto the hood. He clawed at the windshield. Astrid did another wild maneuver and Jeremy catapulted onto the freeway right in front of a speeding eighteen-wheeler. I couldn't stand to look.

"Get off the freeway," Rebecca said, "before the highway patrol comes after us."

I looked back, thinking for sure there'd be a Jeremy-burger smeared all the way across four lanes of traffic, but there was nothing at all.

"Jeremy knows how to take care of himself," said Rebecca. "But he's mad now. He likes to get his own way."

We found ourselves on Ventura Boulevard again, moving slowly back toward home. Mikey was pretty shaken. Astrid was sitting up a little straighter now, and I helped her by moving the seat up as far as it would go.

"Where'd you learn to drive so wildly?" Rebecca said in wonderment.

"Virtual World in Pasadena," Astrid said. "They have a great racing simulator there."

"Thank God for video games," I said.

"You're going to need ammo," said Rebecca. "Look . . . there's a church up ahead. See? St. Eugenia's. They'll have holy water."

Astrid pulled into the parking lot. It was one of those strip-mall churches, looking more like a Pizza Hut than a traditional house of worship.

Rebecca and I left the two younger kids in the car, telling them absolutely *not* to invite anyone inside except us. We went inside—like many churches, it wasn't locked.

"They usually keep the holy water near the front door," Rebecca said. I was glad she knew about this stuff, since no one in my family would have had a clue where to find it.

We found the holy water in a kind of marble basin thing up front, and there was also a big old container of it, with a little spigot, kind of like those metal things they serve coffee out of in cafeterias.

"We don't have anything to put it in," I said.

In the end we wound up taking that whole big metal dispenser thing. We carried it down the steps and started to load it in the backseat of the Cadillac.

"I can't believe you're stealing from a church," Mikey said.

"We'll send them a check," said Astrid.

A wolf was howling. We tensed.

"He's here," Rebecca said.

"We ought to take refuge inside the church," I said, "all of us. Vampires are supposed to be intimidated by churches, aren't they?"

"I don't know about Jeremy," Rebecca said.

"Anyway, I think I'm going to drive now," I said, and Astrid moved over for me. She was shaking. This was wilder than any ride at Magic Mountain, that's for sure. Mikey was huddled in the backseat. I eased the car right up to the front entrance of the church, blocking off the doorway. Then we all snuck back inside. I carried the barrel of holy water on my shoulder, relieved that we weren't actually going to steal it after all.

"Go and hide right behind the altar," Rebecca whispered to the two sixth graders. They scurried up to the railing.

We waited.

There was a knock on the door.

"You're not invited," I said. "Go away."

The door flew open.

"Tough luck," said Jeremy. "You can't *not* invite someone into a church."

He stood there in the glare of the street lights. He seemed so little, so vulnerable, it was hard to believe that he was an ancient predator. He laughed, and shook his head sadly. "Shouldn't mess with me, Johnny," he said. "I won't harm you or your sister; you're wearing the medallions of life. Wouldn't be kosher. But the little geek over there—that's another story."

"Over my dead body," I said.

"If you insist," he said.

All at once he kind of compacted himself into the shape of a wolf. Drooling. Howling. His breath was foul as a corpse. He leaped right at me. I panicked. I heaved the barrel of holy water over my head and brought it smashing down on him. There was a crack.

The wolf was stunned for a moment. The metal kind of buckled and sprang a couple of leaks. As the water dribbled out and hit the wolf's head, it hissed and steamed. The wolf howled again, howled in agony . . . the animal cry started to mutate into the whine of a angry child . . . the wolf started morphing back into Jeremy. Then—as the holy water really started gushing—Jeremy looked up, gazed into my eyes with a tortured, melancholy expression . . . and I saw a single

71

tear form in his right eye and slide in slow motion down his luminous, pale cheek.

Then he exploded.

Everyone was screaming. The holy water turned to mist, and smoke and fog whirled all around us. We all ran out as quickly as we could and dived into the car as mist billowed from the open doorway. I drove away, found the freeway, hightailed it back to the drive-in where, amazingly enough, the horror movie was still going on.

All in all, we had only been gone for fifteen minutes.

Mikey's mother appeared on schedule. We all must have seemed pretty shaken, because the first thing she said was, "Scary movie, huh."

We all nodded. She said, "I always tell Mikey he should stay clear of the gory ones, but he never listens; and he always ends up having nightmares."

She dropped off Astrid, Rebecca and me at my house, then took off; I walked Rebecca home.

Halfway up Tirgoviste, she said, "I don't think I can go through with it, Johnny. Did you see what happened to him? Did you see how he just . . . just blew up?"

"He was evil. He was trying to kill a kid and drink his blood. We did good."

"He was my friend!"

At the front of her house, Trace and Vanina stood on either side of the wrought iron gate, like twin avenging angels, glowering.

"Traitor," Vanina said.

"How could you side with one of them?" said Trace.

"Wait a minute," I said. "I thought you were helping us. Didn't you stall Jeremy?"

"We stalled him," Trace said.

"You *killed* him," Vanina said.

The two of them spread their cloaks to the wind, and flew into the misty night.

We took a few steps down the driveway.

Her dad was standing there. Not wearing sweats this time; he had on a tuxedo, and was every inch a prince of darkness. "I heard about Jeremy," he said.

"Daddy, I—" she began.

"Young lady," he said, "you are grounded until your de-vivification party. You'd better learn just who you are, and why you've been put on this earth."

Well, I got really mad. Rebecca hadn't done anything wrong. She'd gone out on a limb to save someone. "I don't care if you're Count Dracula himself," I shouted at Mr. Teppish. "Your daughter cares about us puny little mortals. She feels what we feel. I love her and you can't make her into a vampire if she doesn't want it. This isn't just picking out the right college, or choosing an elective—her decision's for all time, and you've got no right to make it for her."

Mr. Teppish looked at me for a long time. His demeanor softened. "Don't fight me for her," he said at last. "I meant what I said, when I asked you not to break her heart. Please don't tell her how much you love her, don't write her poems, don't sing her songs. Mortal love is only a fleeting thing. You don't have to carry the bitter residue of it through all those centuries."

I knew that he spoke from experience. The passion that consumed Rebecca's mother must have been some passion. I could see the bitterness in his eyes. I could tell that he loved his daughter, that he was trying to prevent her from getting hurt, but my anger wouldn't go away.

"Go to your room," Mr. Teppish commanded, and Rebecca let go of my hand.

One more lingering look, and she was gone.

CHAPTER NINE

In the Realm of the Spirits

As I tossed and turned, the dream came back to haunt me. The dance. The raven. Other visions too. I thought I saw Jeremy at the window, but now he was your standard B-movie evil kid, with drooling fangs, his flesh rotting off his face, and he was knocking and saying over and over, "Let me in, let me in. . . ."

I woke up. It wasn't light out yet.

Jeremy was standing in the window.

No rotting flesh this time, no fangs dripping with gore. He stood there, just a smiling, chalkfaced little boy, and he said, "Let me in, let me in. . . ."

I'm still dreaming, I told myself. *Mustn't be afraid.*

"Go away," I said. "I killed you."

Jeremy laughed. "You can't kill me," he said. "Not without killing yourself too. Don't you know that I'm your shadow? You can't kill your own shadow."

"No you're not," I said. "You don't belong to any part of me. And I saw you burst into smithereens. I saw you turn into blood-tinged mist."

"That's because you don't know what a vampire really is," said Jeremy. "You have some stupid notion of vampires out of Hollywood and comic books. You think we're like some external, evil force and that you're the good guys and it's some kind of battle for control of the human soul and when you've staked us through the heart it's all over and you go riding into the sunset with the girl. Wrong, bro. So, so wrong. Even Rebecca and those other young 'uns don't understand. They think it's us against them, too. But it's not. We're your dark side, and you're ours. We're your yin and you're our yang. You fit us like a glove. Maybe you did kill me, but that doesn't mean I'm dead."

He didn't scare me. I was more furious than frightened. "Get out of my face," I said.

"It's not enough to pulverize my body. It's not enough to blow me up, cut off my head, incinerate me, shove a red-hot poker through my heart. I'm curled up inside your mind, and you have to dislodge me from there too. I'm the ultimate virus. Go ahead, make me leave, just try."

Wasn't it enough to clobber him with a vat of holy water? This was like one of those endless horror movie series where Jason or Freddy or Michael Myers buys it in some spectacular way and there's *still* a part seven or part eight. I looked around for a weapon, but the only thing I could see was this fancy dancing trophy I'd won at a powwow three years ago— a big old golden horse rearing up and pawing at the air.

It was sitting on top of Astrid's computer printout about Vlad Tepes. I picked it up and kind of swung it and I smashed through the window with it and I could feel the glass cutting my forearm but I didn't care, I just wanted him out of my life. Jeremy spread his cape and howled, and the wind around him howled too, then rushed into my room and everything was totally flying around, the bedsheets, the blankets, the Dracula papers . . . I screamed, just incoherent screaming I guess, but I'm sure I was waking up half the neighborhood.

Jeremy laughed and dissipated into the early morning mist, and I woke up. Again.

The window wasn't smashed, but my wrist sure was bleeding.

Maybe I'd dug my fingernail into it in my sleep. But I was sweating all over and shaking, too. I thought it was an earthquake for a moment but it was only me. I had been unafraid in my dream, but now, in the half-dark, alone in my room, in the deathly stillness, my skin was crawling. I hadn't felt this way since my four-year-old night terrors, I mean I felt like I had to barf and go to the bathroom at the same time but I was too paralyzed to get up and go.

Get a grip! I tried to tell myself. Get a grip!

That's when I heard the drumming.

It was muffled, distant. I thought it was just me, because of how shaky I was feeling, but no, it was definitely coming from somewhere else . . . somewhere echoey, closed off, but not that far away.

Coming from the garage, maybe? My grandfather? Awake at this hour? I looked at my bedside clock, which glowed in the dark, and it was around five or so. I desperately needed someone to talk to. I knew I'd never get back to sleep again. Maybe Grandpa was up and about.

I went out toward the kitchen. There was definitely some kind of drumming, and it was coming from the garage all right. Maybe Grandpa was performing one of those old-time rituals. There was a faint smell of sage in the kitchen even though no one had been cooking. I decided to go check it out.

Grandpa wasn't drumming at all. It was actually a CD— one of those Smithsonian anthropology-type CDS. But he was squatting in the middle of the garage-cum-tipi in full ceremonial regalia, looking as magnificent as a George Catlin painting. There were bundles of sage, and the room was swimming in smoke.

"Hi, *Tunkashila*," I said.

I must have looked pretty stupid by comparison to him, standing there in a pair of Marvin the Martian boxer shorts, still shell-shocked from my encounter with the dream-Jeremy. But he just looked up and said, "Ah, there you are. I see you've chosen the correct attire for the occasion."

"What occasion?" I said.

"You're going to go into the sweatlodge for a while, where you'll purify yourself, and then you're going on a vision quest to encounter the beings from the spirit world who will give you your true identity."

"I am?"

"Well, obviously you are," he said. "Why else would you appear in my tipi at five in the morning in your underwear?"

"But Grandpa, it's not like that at all. I had this awful nightmare and I—"

"Precisely," he said. "You see, the spirit world has a habit of impinging on you when it's time for you to go seek it out."

"There was this vampire and—"

"No doubt he was trying to tell you some important truth about the nature of your existence."

Well, there was no denying that. Maybe there was something to all this.

"Listen, my son," said Grandpa. "You didn't get a bar mitzvah, and you didn't have confirmation, either, and you've gotta have *something* to mark your passage into manhood."

"Can't I just lose my virginity?"

My grandfather laughed. "Always the joker," he said. "Maybe it was the trickster you saw in your dream."

"No, it was Jeremy Weiss."

"Oh," he said. "I've never heard the trickster go by that name before. But hey, this is the nineties."

"Yeah, it is. So I *don't* think I'm gonna be wandering around in the wilderness till I meet some weird animal from the other world, Grandpa. I mean, there's plenty of weird animals around here, but they're all in show business."

"Nineties, shmineties," my grandfather said. "The wilderness is where you find it. You may be walking down the street, having a shake at the mall, Rollerblading along Venice Beach . . . and you'll suddenly find yourself inside the great wilderness of the heart."

Grandpa was talking a lot this morning, and I knew that he meant every word of it, but I was kind of skeptical. Only I was scared, and worried about what was going to happen with Rebecca and the others, and I really needed some old dude to just say, *Johnny, this is how it is, just accept it, believe it, because I know.* So I decided I'd go along with whatever it was Grandpa wanted me to do. I told him so, but he only said, "It's not what I want you to do. You made that decision yourself, by coming to see me."

I didn't want to argue. So I just let him take me to the sweatlodge. Well, it wasn't a sweatlodge exactly—my grandfather had sort of created his modern version of one. It was the guest bathroom, and the first thing he made me do was climb up on the toilet seat and remove the battery from the smoke detector. Then, he showed me these round, flat boulders that he had been heating in the oven overnight, and we lugged them (very carefully, in fireproof dishes) over to the bathtub, where he set the shower on "gentle spring drizzle" and started the steam going. He had already filled the bathroom with magical objects: a buffalo skull, a rattle, and a strange fetish of feathers and human hair, and he had been burning a sage-based incense in the sink.

"You must've been preparing this stuff all night," I said. "How did you know that I was going to do this today?"

"How do you know I don't prepare this stuff every night, just in case you decide to do it?"

He had me there. I sat down on the pink rag rug, wedged between the sink and the bathtub, and breathed in the steam and the sweet fumes. It felt good. Better than a sauna.

"Well, my child," said my grandpa, "stay here for a while."

"How long?"

"Till it's time to come out, of course," he said.

He went back to the garage and came back with a boombox. "The CD is on auto-repeat," he said. "You won't have to touch it."

The sound of drumming and chanting filled the bathroom. He closed the door and I closed my eyes, waiting.

After some time—I don't know how long—I started to feel kind of lightheaded. Hadn't eaten anything that morning, hadn't had enough sleep, the heat was seeping into me, and the sweat was just pouring down my face, my chest, my arms, I don't know, everything was all swimming. I wasn't even sure where I was anymore. The drumming on that CD was echoing in my bones. There were voices on the CD too, wavering and wailing, and though I couldn't understand every word I could feel them driving me on. It was like, take the plunge, let go, don't hold back, just let it all hang loose, no more fear, no more looking back. The voices were in my brain and I couldn't even tell if it was English or Lakota because I guess they were like, speaking in pictures, not even in words.

I didn't even know if my eyes were open or closed. All I know is that the steam was whirling around me and it was more than a bunch of vapors off some hot rocks in a bathtub. It seemed to be coming from deep fissures in the earth . . . the floor and the walls of the bathroom seemed to be growing, transforming . . . into the technicolor crags of the badlands . . . the stark mountainscape of the Black Hills . . . but there was nothing you could fix your gaze on . . . every time I tried to look at something it shifted, morphed, moved to the edge of my vision.

I was standing in the mist but I was still sitting on the floor of the bathroom. I guess you could say that I left my body. In fact, I looked back and sort of saw myself still curled up there . . . like some dead dude . . . not even breathing. I felt that I could float. And then I did. The mist was roiling now and I caught the edge of the mist and was swept along inside it. I was flying but it wasn't the rollercoaster ride of the other night. It was smooth, peaceful, stately.

After a while I spread my arms out and they become like wings. I think, *This is totally cool, I'm an eagle, I'm a hawk.* The sun is filtering through the mist and I catch the light and it propels me. It's beautiful.

But then, abruptly, there's a shadow over the hills. . . .

The raven.

We circle each other. We are wary. I know he is as powerful as I am, maybe a whole lot more. But he's wounded. He flies crooked, and when I get a little closer I see flecks of blood on his left wing. His eyes are the eyes of a dead person.

"Fight me," the raven screeches. "You want the girl? You want your life back? Kill me properly."

I start to descend. I'm not ready to confront the raven yet.

Suddenly I'm standing outside my own bedroom, in the bushes, looking in. There's a bunch of kids sitting on my bed, talking, playing a video game. The one with the controller is Jeremy. But his face is flushed, he's giggling, he looks like flesh and blood. I knock on the window. Trace and Vanina look up at me. They're human, too. "Let me in," I say. But they're trying not to hear me, not to see me. I start banging with my fists, but the glass is hard as stone. And my fists are white and bloodless and cold. . . .

The bathroom door. Someone was banging on it. It flew open and abruptly my spirit was reunited with my body.

S. P. Somtow

Groggily I looked up. It was Rebecca. She kind of threw herself at me and I hugged her. Was this part of my vision too? People are supposed to leave you alone when you're trying to communicate with the realm of the spirits. . . .

"I was having some kind of vision," I said.

"I had to come," she said.

"I thought you were grounded," I said.

"It's daylight," she said. "My dad can't do anything."

"Are we ditching school again?" I said.

"It's Saturday," she said.

Halloween was looming closer. It was tomorrow, in fact, which meant that Grandpa's powwow was tonight.

"I'm sorry for interrupting your . . . whatever this is," she said. "Your grandpa said it was okay, the spirits had nothing else to do, that they can always wait."

"Exactly," my grandfather said, popping in with a robe for me to put on. "You can finish your vision quest later."

He made it sound like my homework, or my lunch.

"I was starting to go somewhere," I said. "It looked like South Dakota."

Grandpa smiled. "I knew you had it in you," he said. "How about some hot cakes?"

CHAPTER TEN

THE POWWOW

We piled into my grandfather's truck (he never liked the BMW, and he'd bought a truck as soon as we arrived in Encino, a battered, secondhand truck which he referred to as *mitashunke*—my horse. There was my grandpa and Astrid in the front, and me and Rebecca squashed in the back with a whole bunch of gear, including several boxes of *Renewing the Hoop* which my grandpa hoped to unload on any unsuspecting New Agers who might wander onto the premises.

The powwow was fifty miles out of town by freeway, at a place called Lancaster, which has a big old fairground. The oddest thing is, you go from our house on the north side of the hill, and you get on the freeway and start going toward Antelope Valley, and in the space of an hour it's like you've traveled halfway across America and a little bit backward in time. Rebecca watched the scenery fly by and I watched her. Now and then, though, I felt myself drifting back into the spirit world, and I could sense the raven's wings beating behind my shoulders.

S. P. Somtow

In the morning light, Rebecca, too, seemed not completely real. She was so pale that the sun seemed to go right through her skin, and when the wind ruffled her hair, it kind of fluttered up and down in waves . . . it was like watching a slow motion relay of reality. She was half-in, half-out of the real world. The city gave way to miles of rocky wilderness, punctuated here and there by a patch of civilization—well, sort of civilization, I mean like, McDonalds and stuff—and it was weird how she was gazing at every little thing, almost like she was saying good-bye to it or something.

"I am," she said to me, and once again I wondered if she was reading my mind.

"Saying good-bye?" I asked her.

"Oh, Johnny, what am I going to do?" she said. She was all crying suddenly, and I didn't know what she wanted me to tell her.

"Well, I could tell you to just say no," I said, "but I know it's a lot more complicated than that."

We pulled into the fairground, where people were just starting to set up. There were about twenty tipis already up. Then there were a whole lot of swap meet booths with jewelry, moccasins, kachina dolls, flutes, drums, pipes, pottery, Navajo rugs, and other knickknacks that people think of as your typical Native American arts and crafts.

Tunkashila parked behind the stalls and we dragged out a big dump bin full of copies of his book and set it up beside the truck. We pinned up a raggedy poster of him in his most Sitting Bull-like pose, and put a life-sized cardboard cutout of him next to the pile of books. Then we set up a chair for him to sit down in, and he did so, crossing his arms and looking just like that old frayed cutout.

Astrid soon found a friend and ran off. Rebecca and I wandered down the row of stalls. She stopped at every one of them, and fingered the jewelry, caressed the baskets and

84

earthenware vessels, or tapped her fingers on the drums. "Did you wear jewelry like this," she asked me, "back in South Dakota?"

"That's Navajo jewelry," I said. It irritates me when people act as if all Indians were the same. It shouldn't bother me by now, but it's a gut thing.

We walked on. "How long till sunset?" she asked me.

"Sunset? It's not even lunchtime yet."

"Why are you so mad at me?"

"I'm not!" I snapped.

"You are, I mean, that thing about the Navajo jewelry. I can't help it if I'm not the most politically correct person in the world, maybe I've got a lot more on my mind than you think, did that ever occur to you?"

"You're the one who pulled me out of the vision thing and—"

"You're the one holding me back from my real nature, did *that* ever occur to you? You're all whining about your identity crisis. Well, my identity crisis is about to get me killed, offered up, desanguinated—you know what that means—it's when they suck out every drop of your blood so they can replace it with the *true* blood. Okay so you've got your vision quests and your sundances, but do you ever have to read about what *we* have to go through, like, in social studies class? At least you can get up and say who you are!"

I didn't really think she was making that much sense. Or if she was, it was all ringing too true for me to want to hear it. We walked on. We didn't walk together, though. We walked Indian style, that is, where each person wanders about, doing his own thing, and yet we somehow end up in the same spot because we've been watching each other out of the corner of our eye. I saw Mr. Mahto, a friend of my grandpa's, and waved to him.

Rebecca kept acting nervous. She kept looking up at the sun. It wasn't bright or anything, but it seemed to bother

her. I wondered why. I mean, it wasn't as if she was a vampire yet. She was still totally human, wasn't she? Was *I* the one flaking? I don't know, but I was having this kind of bases loaded feeling, you know, like when it's all down to me and I'm about to blow it. Maybe it wasn't Rebecca at all.

Then again, she kept hugging herself and shivering, even though it wasn't cold. And after a while she pulled out a pair of mirror shades from her purse and put them on. I couldn't see her eyes then, and that made me a little more mad at her. I couldn't tell if she was looking at me. I couldn't tell what she was thinking. I couldn't tell if she was being cold to me or if she was hiding her feelings. I knew that anything I said would be the wrong thing.

So finally I let her go wander by herself. Maybe I was being a jerk, but I couldn't think straight. It felt so weird being called out of the country of the spirits, and all I really wanted was to get back there and to finish out my vision. I wondered if I was being selfish. I watched Rebecca out of the corner of my eye. She was at the edge of a circle of tipis now, staring at the dancers.

I turned away and went to find my grandpa.

"Abandoning your friend?" he said to me. He was autographing a book for a journalist from the *L.A. Times.*

"Oh!" said the lady, snapping a picture. "You *do* talk."

Grandpa closed his eyes, and he didn't say another word until she walked away, fumbling with a portable tape recorder.

"Is she gone yet?" he asked me.

"Why didn't you at least talk to her?" I said.

"I'm rehearsing for my funeral. You think it's a good day to die?"

"Gimme a break, Grandpa."

"Where's the little lady?"

"Astrid? She's helping some woman bead necklaces."

"No, no, you're deliberately ignoring me. I mean the woman of shadows, the one with one foot in the grave."

"She doesn't have—" I began.

"Are you sure?" said Grandpa. "Maybe for her it's a good day to die."

"She's not going to die. She loves life, *Tunkashila*. I look at her, see her taking in all the colors and the smells and the music of the world. You should have seen her in the back of the truck, like, she was totally drinking in the wind."

"Exactly," said my grandfather. "Like she's trying to say good-bye. I've been doing the same thing for years now. Trouble is, I never seem to quite die."

"Of course not, Grandpa," I said. "You're gonna live for-ever.'" This was making me more and more uncomfortable. "How can she choose death, anyway? Death over me? She loves me."

"Man's gotta do what a man's gotta do," said Grandpa, in a passable imitation of John Wayne. "Okay, so she ain't a man. My point remains."

"Yeah," I said, "but death, death . . . death is one of those one way tickets. You don't just pick death, not voluntarily."

"Who knows if in the country of the dead, folks don't consider themselves the living, and us the dead?"

"Come on, Grandpa, don't lay that ancient Indian wisdom act on me."

He laughed. "I was quoting Euripides. Not a member of the Five Hundred Nations last time I checked."

I walked across the street to the 7–11 to get a Slurpie, then came back and caught up with Rebecca again. She and Astrid had joined a circle of girls and women in a round dance. The circle was bordered by tipis.

The girls stepped slowly, sideways, counterclockwise, fac-ing inward, the circle turning, turning like the earth itself, as the drums pounded out a stately triplet rhythm. I stood on the edge of the circle and waited for them to come around.

"You're not being very nice to her," Astrid said to me, and moved on.

I waited for them to come around again.

I said, "Rebecca, don't go through with it. I need you."

She said, "Love is stronger than death."

I said, "How can it be?"

She said, "Come with me and find out."

She danced beyond the range of conversation. I waited.

"Stay," I said, when she came around again. They did not look at me, she and Astrid, but continued to stare at the circle's center.

"Come," she said.

"Stay," I said.

"Come," she said.

And danced on. Feet apart, feet touching, feet apart, feet touching. It's a simple dance, but it celebrates the great chain of being, the hoop of the universe. It hypnotizes you and after a time you find your heart is throbbing in time to those drumbeats.

The drums kept on pounding. The song wasn't in Lakota, so I couldn't understand any of it, but there were four men banging up a storm and singing in that wheezing, high-pitched way, and the girls kept moving sideways. Some were in deerskin and feathers, some were in street clothes, some were little, some were tall, and all of them circling, circling. And in the heart of the circle was the shadow of a bird.

The shade flitted back and forth. The wings flapped slowly. No real bird could be so big. I looked up. Clouds and sunlight. Nothing there. But it was a nothing whose presence cast darkness over the grass.

"Why don't you dance, too, Johnny?"

"Didn't bring my gear."

"Afraid to dance?"

"No. Just didn't bring my gear."

But a few guys were in the circle now. Bells jangled on their wrists and feet. They were pretty good even though some of them were kind of potbellied, nothing like those George Catlin paintings you see in the museum; sleek, defined, fierce-faced braves from the past. They shook and they wiggled and they raised their fists and I knew that this was supposed to be a good thing, a celebration of where we all came from, but I didn't really feel it at first. It just looked like some aging fat dudes huffing and puffing in ill-fitting clothes. Rebecca now, she looked different from the rest of the girls who moved in that stately circle around the guys. She didn't seem to see the real world, or feel the dusty breeze and the flat California sunlight. She could see another world.

Maybe she's right to want to leave all this behind, I thought. I mean, I didn't feel there was much to like about the world right then.

When Rebecca circled past again, she said, laughing, "Why don't you dance?"

The drums kept on banging away. Slow and steady, the pulse of the earth itself. I could feel my feet working themselves into the rhythm, all by themselves almost . . . left toes left heel right toes right heel left toes left heel right toes right heel . . . I don't really know how I broke through the circle but suddenly, there I was, right in the center, and they were wheeling around and around me and suddenly I could understand every word they were singing . . . over and over . . . a song of love and saying good-bye . . . the girls were circling faster and faster. Something was going on. They were whirling so fast they seemed to be in flames. There was a lot of smoke. Or maybe mist. It was rolling in over the ground. Pouring down from the sky. The girls were a blur now. It was like one of those carnival rides where you're spinning and spinning and it's like you're falling down the middle of the world's largest kaleidoscope. The drumbeats grew louder. I could still see Rebecca. She was part of the circle yet not part of it. Somehow she was suspended in the air, looking in at me, the only thing that wasn't moving. Her cheeks were moist. She was about to cry, but the light was slowly draining from her eyes.

Suddenly I realized that my grandfather was right. I'd been too wrapped up in myself to see that she really was torn between me and death.

I heard the beating of great wings. I knew that the raven was wheeling overhead. His shadow crept over Rebecca's face, like the shadow of the moon stealing over the sun, stealing the light, stealing the warmth, plunging us all into deepest night.

Tunkashila was right about something else too. It didn't matter if I was hunched up in the restroom in a cloud of steam or just walking down the street. When it's time to have your vision, it finds you. There's no running away.

I was dancing up a storm in the middle of a circle of tipis and parked trucks, in a fairground somewhere near Los Angeles, but I was also all alone, dancing, at the center of the great circle of the universe.

CHAPTER ELEVEN

THE DANCE OF LIFE AND DEATH

So there I was, inside the circle of flesh and blood, and also inside the circle of my own soul. And the space around me starts to stretch and warp and bend, and all the faces have a rainbow fringe around them.

Time twists in on itself. Past and future become present. I don't know how it happens but my street clothes have been melting away and there are heavy anklets on my bare feet and buckskin leggings and a long mane of eagle feathers in my hair. I feel the wind against my chest. I feel the dry paint on my cheeks, feel my sweat as it seeps from my pores to fill the cracks in the pigment. There are silver bands around my arms. I feel the weight of them and I'm thinking, silver, silver, keep away the vampires.

The drumbeats are the heartbeats. The wall of smoke and fire is the steam in the sweatlodge and the fire in my blood. I'm with all these people and I'm completely alone, in a wilderness more desolate than the badlands of my childhood. I see Rebecca in the distance but it's only a reflection or something.

At least she still casts a reflection. . . .

The wings of the raven are beating. There's someone here with me, I realize suddenly. It's my own shadow. But it's more than a shadow because it seems to have its own will, its own life.

I leap. He crouches. I turn left. He turns right. He's a dark mirror to my thoughts. I spread my arms. My wings are feathered and broad and they catch the cold wind. I'm an eagle and when I leap up I leave the ground completely and begin to soar. But I can't shake the shadow no matter what. He clings to me. He's heavy, too. He's trying to pull me down to earth. The shadow's growing, too. His wings are sleek and black, and he's creeping over the disk of the sun just the way he eclipsed the light from Rebecca's face.

I think he wants to swallow up the world. I'm afraid of him. I guess I have to fight him or something. Isn't that what's supposed to happen in these vision things? Every movie has a scene where the hero faces down his shadow. I know what I have to do. The wings are hard to take. I flap once or twice, try to get the hang of them. They work better when you open wide and kind of let the wind grab you, but to do that you have to surrender a little, you have to trust where the wind wants to take you.

The wind wants me to fly higher and the shadow wants to drag me down. But I'm still rising. I'm pushing through the ceiling of the world, piercing the highest layers of cloud. It's bitterly cold. I think it's snowing. There's still no sunlight, no matter how high I go. At length I come to roost.

I see Rebecca—

Standing on the landing at the top of that twisted turret that rises up from the house on Tirgoviste Lane. The tower has pushed through the clouds too, like the beanstalk in the fairy tale. The wind is blowing her hair behind her and she's even more pale than ever. I start to float toward her over the billowing carpet of cloud. She's beautiful and I want to

be with her with the kind of desperate longing that only a teenager can feel. I have the hang of steering now so I flap my wings a couple of times—I still feel a bit stupid doing this but I figure that I'm dreaming anyway so I might as well go with the flow—and in a moment I'm hovering above her, calling to her.

"Rebecca, Rebecca. . . ."

I can hear her speaking, but she doesn't seem to be talking to me in particular. She says, "I hear something. I don't know what it is."

"Rebecca—"

"I wonder if it's only the wind. The windows of the old house creak a lot. Like in the old house, back in Romania, when I was just a little girl."

I do hear the hinges of windows squeaking, and the ancient house settling on its foundations, making those murmuring sounds that only old buildings make. Doesn't she see me at all? I settle on the landing, reach out to her over the rusty railings.

She goes on muttering to herself, seeing right through me. I get the feeling she's dreaming too. Maybe she danced herself into a trance at the powwow. She says, "Gotta get back downstairs, gotta get ready, gotta stop thinking about all the other stuff."

I reach out. Touch her shoulder as she turns away from me.

She winces. "Who's there?" she says aloud. Then, to herself, "Nervous. All jumpy. Go back down." And she starts to go down the steep, spiral stairway that leads back down into her house. I follow her unseen.

The mist follows us down so I know that I'm still inside the territory of dream. Now and then I try to attract Rebecca's attention again, but she doesn't see me.

*   *   *

Rebecca walks down a corridor lined with ancient portraits. Some of them seem to be the Draculas of Hollywood—Lugosi, Lee, Langella—and others, wild and fearsome creatures with pointed ears and fanged incisors, like in that old silent movie *Nosferatu, the Vampire,* which sometimes comes on PBS. The mist wraps itself around us. Her footsteps are echoey, and the air is cold and clammy.

She turns a doorknob. I guess this is her bedroom. I've never been here—Astrid has—but in some ways it's a typical bedroom of a sixteen-year-old girl. There's a computer, and a screen saver shows endless black cats, chasing one another and an unravelling ball of yarn. There's a dressing table with an ornate mirror, all gilt, with little Cupids fluttering around the frame, and she sits down in front of it and starts to brush her hair, and I can't help saying something to her even though I realize she doesn't know I'm here. . . .

"If you can see yourself in a mirror," I say, "no way are you a vampire."

She's so startled she drops the brush. "Johnny!" She whirls around but I'm nowhere to be seen. Then she turns back and you know what it is? She sees a ghostly me, inside of that mirror, staring from a shroud of mist. And I look too, and I see me, but not the me at the fairground, leaping and whooping, not the me with the great wings soaring through the clouds. It's the me in the sweatlodge that's really a bathroom in the 'burbs, and I'm all hollow-eyed and drenched in sweat. So maybe I've never really left that place. Maybe she never interrupted me. Maybe I never went to the powwow. Maybe all those things are dreams within dreams.

"Have you come to talk me out of it?" Rebecca said. It was feeling less and less like a dream now and more and more like reality. Because the way she talked, it really was her, I mean it wasn't some reverberating dream-voice. Again I wasn't sure if I was in my vision or out of it.

"I don't know. I kind of thought there'd be like this great

battle for your soul, that I'd have to, you know, wrestle your dad for possession of it or something."

"Men don't 'possess' me, Johnny. I own myself."

"So this is it? Tomorrow's your big day but you thought you'd have one big fling with a mortal dude before you kiss your life good-bye?"

"It's not like that at all," Rebecca said.

"Then why do I feel like the girl who pops out of the cake at the bachelor party?"

"It wasn't supposed to be like that," she said. "It was my dad's idea, I admit. He's all, 'You have to be really sure, Rebecca. I can't *make* you choose the undead over the living. Why don't you go out, get a boyfriend, live like a human being for a while, check it out? That's why we moved here.' Bad timing, though. Why couldn't Dad have thought of it earlier?"

"Seems to me like he was rushing you through this part. Didn't want you to become too attached. He told me not to break your heart, did you know that?"

"How could you break my heart?" she said. "I hardly know you. We've been together less than a week. How could he say a thing like that? How could he know something like that?" And she began to weep. Bitterly. As if there was no tomorrow. Even though she knew as well as I did that there would be a tomorrow, if she really wanted to rebel, if she really wanted to choose me.

And that's what I said to her. "I want you to tell them no," I said. "Can't you do that for me?"

"I—I could, but—"

"Okay, we're only sixteen, maybe life doesn't last forever. Maybe love's like a candle and any little gust can put it out. But you're not even giving it a chance. Sure I was mad at you at the powwow and I was like totally selfish and not thinking about the things you're going through. But that's part of love too, getting mad at each other, making up . . . quarreling in evening, sending flowers in the morning. . . ."

"You make it sound like a movie," she said sadly.

"And speaking of movies, we've never even watched a movie together from beginning to end. We've never spoken on the phone for seven hours about nothing. We've never been to Disneyland to make fun of the tourists. We've only had a few moments here and there, snatched from between other things. But even from those moments I know that I have to have more. I need you, Rebecca. I mean, what if the candle doesn't blow out? What if these feelings we have for each other are like, deeper than we can imagine? What if we find out, after being together for, I don't know . . . a month . . . a year . . that we might want to sit around being old together?"

"You're just making me cry even more," she said, and she really was, I mean she was all puffy and blowing her nose on a wad of tissues. And my image in the mirror was blurring, too. I guess that I was seeing myself through her eyes, and if my reflection was blurred by tears, that's what was in the mirror.

"So you'll do it. Say you'll do it."

"I'll do it," she said. She didn't sound that convinced, but that was all I had to cling to.

She kissed the reflection in the mirror. It was all misted over and my face was just a smear of color on the shiny surface. When her lips touched the mirror I felt cold air against my cheek. I tried to embrace her, but I knew that all she could feel was the wind.

There was a knock on the door. . . .

First there was Vanina, in a floor-length leather coat, black lipstick, and a black heart painted on each cheek. "Rebecca," she said, "like, you're a mess!"

I tried to hide behind the bed, but it was obvious that Vanina couldn't see me at all, so I got bold and kind of crept out to sit there, leaning against the headboard. Vanina sat down right next to me.

"I didn't know the sun had set already," Rebecca said.

"Oh, barely," said Vanina. "but I had to be here right from the start. Here, let me get that for you." She pulled a handkerchief from an inside pocket, and began dabbing at Rebecca's eyes. "There, there," she said. "It'll all be over soon."

"What if I'm making the wrong decision?" Rebecca looked as though she might start crying again any minute.

"Oh, don't worry about the second thoughts. Like, we all have them. It's okay. I mean, Trace totally wanted to be a brain surgeon when he grew up. He's seen plenty of brains since then, though. If you know what I mean."

"Scrambled, mashed, diced, over easy," said a young male voice, and I saw that Trace was sliding in under the doorway. It was disturbing how they could be paper-thin one minute and normal-looking the next. He was wearing a tuxedo, and a safety pin through his left earlobe. He looked every inch a vampire. He sat down on the other side of me. They both looked straight through me. "Brains are my favorite."

"Not much blood in one, though," Vanina said.

"But the texture is unforgettable. Full-bodied. A little dry. Like a fine wine. Not that I ever drink wine," he added in a cheezy Bela Lugosi voice.

Rebecca burst into tears again.

Vanina and Trace exchanged a look.

"Jungle fever," Trace said.

"It's that mortal, isn't it?" said Vanina. "The one with the really interesting eyes. Big blue eyes and a kind of chocolaty complexion . . . very yummy. Part Indian or something. Type O, if my nasal memory serves me right."

"If you want him that bad," Trace said, "just say the

word. He's gonna be sixteen, right? We'll do him tonight if you want. You can be each other's birthday present."

"Don't talk that way, Trace," said Vanina. "You know the rules. No more involuntary vampires. A vampire who never wanted to be a vampire is not a happy camper. Very unpleasant creatures they are. Too many of them knocking around from the bad old days."

"Yeah," said Trace, "he has to *want* to change."

"You could probably talk him into it, though. The way he was looking at you . . . poor little puppy."

Rebecca didn't say anything. She just looked in the dressing table mirror now and then, and she could see that I was still around, listening to every word.

Vanina said, "Then again, I don't think I could get used to having him around, hanging out with us. I mean, think about what he did to Jeremy."

"Yeah," said Trace, "Jeremy's in a jillion pieces, scattered to the four winds, and he was one of the Old Ones . . . what nerve."

Rebecca said, "Well, how was he to know that? We all look alike to them."

"Are you defending a human being?" Trace said.

"You might as well be defending a bag of french fries," said Vanina, and picked at the corner of her lip with a finger. "Is my lipstick okay?" she said. "Sometimes it *is* a pain never being able to look in a mirror. . . ."

"Jeremy was so looking forward to tonight," Trace said. "It's just a crying shame."

The room grew suddenly darker. Then a low rumble, sort of like in a movie theater with really fresh Dolby. Puffs of smoke. Little whorls of rainbow lightning. Something . . . someone was materializing in the middle of the room . . . weaving himself together from a million filaments of cold light . . . Jeremy. All at once he was there, nude, blue-gray, like a corpse in a morgue.

Vanina whisked off the bedspread and threw it over him. For all that, they didn't really seem very surprised to see him. When eternity stretches ahead of you, I guess you get pretty jaded.

"Thanks," Jeremy said, wrapping himself in the dark purple satin and struggling to his feet. "I thought I'd never make it back. It's tough, finding your way back from the place beyond."

The place beyond . . . I remembered how Rebecca had talked about it before. The place that was to vampires what eternity is to mortals. The place that Timmy Valentine was supposed to have gone to.

As if on cue, I heard the intro from one of Timmy Valentine's earliest hits from somewhere downstairs. Pre-grunge, but it had a raw edge to it, with the vampire rock star's voice adding a kind of sweetness, like a lump of sugar in a cup of espresso.

"They're testing out the sound system for your party," Vanina said. "I hope it's not *all* going to be proto-neo-Gothic music. Something new would be nice. Your dad says that the Senseless Vultures are going to drop in, in person."

"It's all just a charade," Jeremy said. "We should just get it over with now."

"Yeah," Vanina said. "C'mon, Rebecca, we're your friends. All that stuff with the official desanguination, the ritual words, your father giving you away like you're gonna get married . . . it's not real. We could do it here, just me and Trace and Jeremy . . . the people who really care about you."

"We'll even do the Raitt kid, if you really want us to," Trace said. "Now *that's* real friendship."

"I bet you invited him to your coming-out party, didn't you?" said Vanina. "Maybe we can arrange a double initiation. That'd be cool. I've never seen one of those."

"Don't be stupid," Trace said. "He'd never show up without a silver ankh around his neck. We'll have to get him before he leaves. Maybe we can go trick-or-treating."

I shuddered.

"Well, I am not 'doing the Raitt kid', as you put it," Jeremy said. "Allow me at least a modicum of good old-fashioned hate, guys. This *boy*, who knows nothing, has seen nothing, understands nothing, just smashes me to smithereens for no damn reason, sends me beyond, and if I weren't so ancient and powerful I'd still be beyond right now, forever and ever, amen. If I could get my hands on him right this very minute, I'd—"

Jeremy stopped himself. He looked straight at where I was sitting. *Oh God*, I thought, *he's seen me, he really has.*

It was only for a split second. He saw something, I know he did. He wasn't sure of it. For a moment he wasn't his cocky self. Abruptly, he turned, churned himself into mist, and started funneling himself out through the keyhole.

Vanina said, "Well, why don't you finish dressing," and leaped off the bed . . . suddenly she was a black cat, hissing, pawing the carpet before dashing off.

"See you downstairs," Trace said, and sort of melted away.

"Remember," I'm telling her. "You promised. You gave me your word. You're not going to go through with it."

"It's not fair!" Rebecca says. "Why do I have to be the one to give up my identity? Why aren't you agreeing to come with me? Why is it always the guy who comes storming in to save the girl?"

"I don't know." I remember the taste of blood, that first big headrush at the Café Transylvania. That's what this vision quest is really about, I guess. Whether to stay human or not. It is all so complicated not because I've been on the outside looking into their world, seeing their point of view. And I am attracted to their world, I really am. I know now that we all have a craving for dark things sometimes. "It's not about rescuing damsels in distress, though, I've learned that." I'm thinking of the dance, the circle of woman, the leaping of man. I can hear the drumbeats once more, and I'm starting to fade out of this reality. . . .

"I guess I'll see you at the party," she says.

"Can you try kissing me again?"

We throw our arms around each other's emptiness. We kiss the chill air. The mirror runs with reflected tears.

I vanish from her view, and I find myself adrift again, floating through clouds of smoke and steam. . . .

CHAPTER TWELVE

HALLOWEEN XVI

I opened my eyes. They were all crusted over. It took a long time to understand that I was back in the world. The sweet smell of sage filled my nostrils. Slowly I got up and rubbed my eyes and toweled myself off a little. The real world felt strange to me at first. The colors weren't as bright. The sounds—my grandfather's drumming CD pouring from a boombox, my sister clattering around in the kitchen somewhere out of sight, and the *drip-drip-hiss-hiss* of water onto the hot stones in the bathtub—they all seemed to come from an immeasurable distance at first. Gradually I came down to earth all the way. My temples were still throbbing when I came out of the bathroom, wrapped in a Mickey Mouse beach towel, drying my hair with a washcloth.

I went into the den, where Grandpa was watching *Oprah*. "How was it?" he asked me.

"Wild," I said.

"You entered the country of the spirits?"

"Yeah . . . I guess."

"And a spirit animal came to guide you through the wilderness?"

"Sort of. Well, it wasn't an animal . . . it was kind of my own shadow. Or maybe it was a raven. I don't know. And then I talked to Rebecca, except that she couldn't see me. But that was in the middle of the powwow."

"You've had a great vision, kid. The powwow hasn't even started yet. Astrid's still helping me load up the truck."

"It wasn't anything like I thought it would be. You were totally right about one thing, though, when you said that maybe in the land of the dead people think that *they're* alive, and that to them, we are the dead. . . ."

"That's a very wise thing to say, son, but I don't remember saying it."

"You quoted Euripides."

"Euripides? What tribe did he belong to?"

"He was a Greek, Grandpa. One of those ancient dudes."

"Euripides pants, Eumenides," my grandfather quipped.

Too late I remembered that the whole conversation where *Tunkashila* had said all that had actually been inside my vision. And yet I got the feeling that Grandpa was somehow having a little joke at my expense. To an old-time Lakota like my grandpa, dreams are as real as the real world. If we'd had a conversation in the other world, it was as valid as if we'd been doing lunch at the mall. Never did quite understand how that worked. I mean, what if two people had contradictory dreams about each other?

"That only happens to the *washichus*," said Grandpa. Was it telepathy, or did he just know me too well? "On the other hand, you're half *washichu* yourself. You understand the way white people think; I don't."

"Grandpa, did Rebecca come by the house earlier? Did she somehow slip into my vision?"

"Can't talk about those things," he said. "Visions are private."

But I had to talk about it. In my vision I had touched the edge of a great truth. I needed to share it. "It's not what I thought at all, though," I said. "She wasn't a maiden and I wasn't a knight in shining armor. I wasn't an angel of light battling the Jeremy of darkness to save her. I kind of expected it to be that way . . . you know, good versus evil, a psychedelic version of *Star Wars* . . . but it wasn't that at all."

"So explain," said Grandpa.

"This is what I learned," I said. "Life and death are partners in a dance. Like light and dark. Like man and woman, too, I guess. In the old Indian way the women are the steady ones, the slowly moving circle of the earth, and the men are the leaping ones in the middle, and maybe that's kind of a male chauvinist viewpoint but however you look at it it's one dancing with the other and you can't separate them because this dance is what makes the universe revolve. It makes time exist, and all the things we value, like love and courage and hope and compassion, happen inside of time. All the things we are scared of too. Everything is in that dance. It's the creation and the destruction of the world. Okay? But those vampires . . . it's like they're refusing to dance. They won't join in. They want to be outside it. One of the things that makes life so exciting, that makes the colors and the sights and sounds so rich, is that I know I'm gonna die one day. They don't know that. That's why the way they live is all one endless gray."

"You should have told all this to your mother," said my grandfather. "You too could be a best-selling New Age author without ever writing a single word."

"Grandpa—"

He chuckled. I wasn't really mad at him, just relieved, mostly, that I had made it through in one piece.

The next thing was that Mom called from Mexico to say she'd be back in a couple of days, and to wish me a happy birthday, and then Grandpa let me drive the truck to the

105

DMV to take my driver's test, which I flunked. But hey. There was always tomorrow.

Then we went to the powwow, sold hundreds of autographed books even though my grandpa didn't speak, I dusted off all the old dancing clothes and won a junior trophy for my fancy dancing, and we made it home in time for Astrid to go trick-or-treating, which she did in a Ronald Reagan mask.

It was Halloween number sixteen for me, and for the first time I really felt too old. Last year, in South Dakota, I still felt like a kid. Today I had the big party at Castle Dracula to go to, and I stood in front of the mirror in my bathroom trying on about a dozen different neckties. They all belonged to Astrid's dad—you know, the Norwegian—and I thought they all looked pretty stupid. So I ended up not dressing up for it at all, just wearing a pair of black denims and a black T-shirt. Black, at least, was appropriate. I mean, like, it *was* a funeral, in a way.

I Rollerbladed through streets full of giggling children— a Freddy Krueger or a Jason in every gaggle, and a few more traditional monsters too, mummies and ghosts and vampires. Pumpkins in the doorways. All except one front gate; no pumpkin at the house on Tirgoviste.

I showed up with the invitation in one hand, slipping the silver ankh around my neck as I walked up the driveway. There was a pumpkin here after all, though you couldn't see it from the street. Someone had put little wheels on it, made it look like a carriage, and tied two rubber mice to the front of it.

Rebecca opened the door for me herself. She wore black, but it was sort of a wedding dress, all lace and frills and bows, with a bright red rose pinned to her bosom. She looked at me shyly. I could hear the crowd milling around, beyond the foyer, but I didn't go in yet.

"Is that the Cinderella pumpkin?" I said.

She laughed. "Maybe someone's idea of a joke. But it's kind of true, isn't it? I am Cinderella, and soon it'll be midnight, but there won't be any glass slipper. . . ."

"No," I said, "I guess not."

"I had the strangest dream," Rebecca said softly.

"I know," I said.

She clasped my hands and drew me into the house. I'd only been in the back way before, and had never seen the magnificence of this anteroom, with its baroque chandeliers and its life-sized painting of Vlad the Impaler glaring down over the marble bust of a Roman goddess.

I explained, "My grandfather believes that everything that happens in dreams is as real as the real world. Do you think it's true? 'Cause you were in my dream, and you could only see me in a mirror, and we tried to kiss, but it was like hugging the wind."

"Oh, Johnny," said Rebecca, "after tonight I'll never dream again—" and this time she did embrace me. There was still warmth in her. She made me tingle. She kissed me, but after only a second her lips grew cold, and she pulled back. "There, Johnny," she said, "you've sucked the last bit of humanness out of me."

"I do love you," I said.

"I know," she said, "but in a few months, in a year, you'll be going out with someone, I'll fade from your thoughts. But it won't be the same for me. The ache will be forever. We don't choose what we are."

I couldn't answer that, couldn't say anything that would make things better for us. I wanted to scream at her, "Of course you can choose, it's human to be able to choose . . ." but I knew it wouldn't do any good. So I just followed her into the reception room.

There's not really much I can say about the party. A great mahogany coffin was set up in the middle of the room. There

107

were only about fifty guests, but at least some of them were like, really big celebrities. I guess when you live that long, you get connections. Although everyone was wearing black, you could tell the human beings by their silver amulets. I recognized Tygh Simpson, lead singer of the Senseless Vultures, but I knew it would be kind of fannish to ask him for his autograph. He was talking to Caressa Byrd, a famous romance writer who had recently started doing vampire books—well, romantic vampire books, you know, girl meets vampire; Astrid and her friends love those sort of stories— and she was wearing a killer cocktail dress a couple sizes too small. She had a glass of champagne and each time she laughed it looked like she was going to split a seam. I thought I caught a glimpse of Timmy Valentine, but I couldn't be sure. Not that I was going to call the *Enquirer* to report another sighting of the vanished rock star, anyways. There was even a talk show host, and I realized he was probably doing research for a show on "women who think they're vampires" or something like that.

Then there were the kids. Vanina and Trace and I guess Jeremy, though I knew now that he was no kid. They sort of swooped down on Rebecca and swept her away from me, and she looked back at me for a moment; but I couldn't tell if it was with pity or with regret.

I sat down on a stuffy couch all by myself and let the party kind of swirl around me.

Finally they had the ceremony, and it went like this: Rebecca's father gave a long speech about the history of vampires. You know, it wasn't that different from the history of any people with long memories and old traditions. I've heard similar stories from Grandfather, and from my Jewish relatives too. Persecution. Being driven from country to country, never finding a home . . . coming to America, struggling to survive. People listened politely, but it was something they'd all heard a million times, I guess, because the only ones who

108

seemed interested were the humans. Rebecca's dad didn't mention the one big difference—that vampires can't continue to be around much, unless they feed on us.

So finally what happened was that Rebecca lay down on sort of an altar, and this big dude in black robes slit her left wrist—I guess maybe they drugged her or something, because she didn't seem to be in pain—and her blood slowly dripped into like a big old crystal sconce. And meanwhile, all the vampires stood in line where a woman was standing with a jeweled goblet, and each one of them pricked a finger or made a little slit in his wrist and donated a little bit of blood. Except for Vlad, who had like a mean-looking dagger and plunged it into his own heart, all the way to the hilt, and held the goblet to his chest. It was scary but I couldn't look away. A human being dies and there'd be gore flying everywhere, but even Mr. Teppish's heart had only a few drops to give, and they were viscous and purplish-black, more like molasses than blood.

He pulled out the dagger and everyone applauded.

Then he went to his daughter and, with great tenderness, held the goblet to her lips while she drank. Meanwhile, the sconce was filling up quickly, and I guess Rebecca passed out or something, and they were passing it around, and all the vampires were drinking, taking deep draughts, sighing. It was the sighing that made my hair stand on end. They sounded like a pack of wolves after a satisfying dinner. I fingered the silver ankh and wondered if one of them would forget himself and attack me.

Everybody said a few words about Rebecca. Her father spoke of her mother, and about being literally consumed by passion. Trace and Vanina talked about the pleasant nights they'd had together at the Café Transylvania. Jeremy got up and said, "Rebecca almost got me killed the other night. You know, for her, I might even have considered it. . . ."

I thought it was only vampires who would be allowed to

speak, but last of all, Mr. Teppish took me up to where she was lying, and asked me if I wanted to say something.

"Oh, I really couldn't," I said. "I'm not a vampire."

"But she loved you," Mr. Teppish said.

"Okay, Vlad," I said. I didn't even mind calling him that. We did have a kind of bond, he and I, although he was a thousand years old and I was only sixteen. "I should be mad at all you guys," I said to all of them, "because you're taking her away from me. Or maybe I should be saying, hey, take me too. But this isn't *Romeo and Juliet*. It's real life. I can't give up being human. Rebecca couldn't give up her friends, her family, her place in the world of darkness. I thought it'd be cool to have kids, grow old together, and all that crap, but then, when I think of the day we visited Trace and Vanina's tomb in that old ruined cemetery . . . I can see us, when we're old, driving down to that cemetery again, and I can see her face, knowing that her friends are in there still, and still young, not a wrinkle on their faces, untouched by everything we've lived through. I'm sure she thinks about that too. Maybe it's not worth giving up everything for the sake of one person you've just met, who, maybe, isn't even the right one. I'll never know. Good-bye, Rebecca." I kissed her ice-cold cheek.

They lowered Rebecca into the coffin and closed the lid. The crystal sconce had been completely drained, and Mr. Teppish took and smashed it over the lid of the coffin. A servant swept the pieces into a porcelain urn, and carried it outside.

Then the coffin was loaded into a hearse, and we all trooped down to the crypt where Vanina and Trace are buried, where a brand-new mausoleum had been put up—seemingly overnight—to hold Rebecca.

We said good-bye to the vampires—we mortals, I mean—because I guess that was one of their traditions, that only those of her kind would watch over the grave until the moments before sunset. Another old tradition, dating from the time when vampire hunters with stakes would roam the graveyards. So I didn't see her rise up, didn't see her greet the darkness, didn't see her draw first blood from a living creature.

I came home around midnight. It was about the strangest sixteenth birthday a guy could have. The house was quiet and dark. I almost tripped over little piles of Halloween candy that littered the floor.

I went to bed, and I didn't dream that night.

CHAPTER THIRTEEN

FINDING MYSELF

Today I woke up and I decided I'd go down to Rebecca's grave.

Mom's home from Mexico now, along with a new boyfriend, Bob, who seems okay, though I'm probably going to withhold judgment until he shows me he has staying power. I passed the driver's test the third time around—Bob actually helped me out, but maybe he's just buttering me up while he takes Mom for a ride, so I don't trust him yet—and now I have the use of Grandpa's truck whenever I need it.

Grandpa "talked" so well at the big Beverly Hills autograph bash that he landed a seven-figure contract for a three-book deal. Unfortunately, he's stopped talking again. Says he'll talk next summer, when him and me drive all the way back to Pine Ridge and spend a few months teaching me all that ancient wisdom stuff.

Well okay, so I drove down to the grave this morning, before school. I cleared away the garlic from Vanina and

Trace's monument—I still do that for old times' sake, sometimes.

Then I went down to Rebecca's crypt. I have a key. It came in the mail a few days after Rebecca's coming out party, with a note from her father, which read:

> Thanks—I think....
> —V.X. Teppish

There's a crystal vase at the foot of the coffin. I filled it with water from the thermos I brought with me, and I replaced the red rose that I'd left there last week with a brand new one. It takes them no time at all to wither. Just like human beings. But I'll go on doing this for a while. I like to think that when she wakes up each sunset, she'll know that she still has a link to the mortal world.

Sunset came and I drove over to Aunt Hannah's house for *shabbes*. Since the experience with Rebecca I haven't really minded seeing my mom's many Encino relatives. So today, they were doing all those traditional things that they usually do, and I volunteered to say the prayer over the bread, and I got it all right, which impressed the crap out of them.

So Mom said, "Does that mean that you've made a choice now?"

"About what?" I said, trying to avoid the subject.

Aunt Hannah, who is very much more overbearing than my mother, said, "Well, you have to decide who you are, don't you? You can't remain your whole life in some kind of ethnic limbo. You have to choose."

"I've already chosen, Aunt Hannah," I said. "I choose to be human."

"Oh, rubbish," she said "You know very well what we mean."

So I got up at the table, and I said to the whole pack of them, "I'm a mutt, and I'm proud to be a mutt."

Then my mom said, "You know, Hannah, he's right. I never had the guts to say it to *my* parents when they got into a lather about me marrying a Lakota Indian. They kept telling me that my fixation with this 'noble savage thing' was just a phase I was going through. Well, it looks like I did one thing right. Johnny, I'm proud of you for saying it, and let's all drink to it."

There was wine all around, and clinking glasses, and toasts, and all that, but when the bottle came in my direction, I said softly, "I nevairr drink . . . wine," in my best Bela Lugosi voice.

Only Astrid laughed.

At night, sometimes, she comes to my window. Like tonight. She's more beautiful than ever, if you can imagine that. Her skin is like moonlight, and her eyes glisten, and her hair just billows about her features as she gazes at me, a half-smile on her rosy lips, always melancholy.

"Oh, Johnny, Johnny, let me in," she whispers to me, sometimes when I'm dreaming, sometimes when I'm half in, half out of slumber.

But I never do.

It's not that I don't care. But I know that the apparition outside my window isn't really Rebecca. It was the spark of life that I loved in Rebecca, and this Rebecca is a walking corpse, Rebecca's shell, without Rebecca's soul. I do tell myself this, and every time she comes I am still tempted to open the window, to let her carry me away to dark oblivion.

But I don't.

In time she will go away. She used to come every night, but now it's much less often. I'm starting to think that she never came to my window, that they were all dreams . . .

but then, like my *tunkashila,* I know that dreams can tell the truth.

She told me my feelings would fade. But I don't think they'll ever die. She was the first girl that I ever loved. In a way, I'm all that's left of her. She's part of me always, Rebecca Teppish, the vampire's beautiful daughter.